## When the Clock Strikes Thirteen

**Ruskin Bond** has been writing for over sixty years, and now has over 120 titles in print—novels, collections of short stories, poetry, essays, anthologies and books for children. His first novel, *The Room on the Roof*, received the prestigious John Llewellyn Rhys Prize in 1957. He has also received the Padma Shri (1999), the Padma Bhushan (2014) and two awards from Sahitya Akademi—one for his short stories and another for his writings for children. In 2012, the Delhi government gave him its Lifetime Achievement Award.

Born in 1934, Ruskin Bond grew up in Jamnagar, Shimla, New Delhi and Dehradun. Apart from three years in the UK, he has spent all his life in India, and now lives in Mussoorie with his adopted family.

GW00371966

# RUSKIN BOND

## When the Clock Strikes Thirteen

RUPA

Published by
Rupa Publications India Pvt. Ltd 2017
7/16, Ansari Road, Daryaganj
New Delhi 110002

*Sales centres:*
Allahabad Bengaluru Chennai
Hyderabad Jaipur Kathmandu
Kolkata Mumbai

ISBN: 978-81-291-4879-7

First impression 2017

10 9 8 7 6 5 4 3 2 1

Printed at Nutech Print Services, New Delhi

# CONTENTS

# INTRODUCTION

Fiction is what comes to rescue when our real lives become too monotonous. At least for me that has always been so. It could be a simple story about a neighbour, or about a panther that has an entire village terrified, or the experience of being in a haunted mansion one stormy night—my imagination has always run wild with fiction.

In this book I have collected a few of my fiction works— some humorous, some scary, some anticlimactic and some gentle ones. Rest assured, I promise to keep you engaged through each of them. Besides, it would be difficult for even you to not pay attention when you read about Mangal Singh, the dacoit, holding Inspector Hukam Singh and Sub-inspector Guler Singh captive and how their story meets an unlikely end.

I hope to entertain you with the story of Rani Ma who dreams of dying when the clock strikes thirteen one day, and until then enjoys her drinks alone. I am certain that you will be curious to know what happens in the end of 'Will Astley Return?' when Robert Astley goes far, far away, leaving behind his loyal servant, Prem Bahadur, to take care of his house. Years pass and Prem continues to wait for Astley to return one day... But does he return?

I have also put in this collection the gentle story of Bina, who shifts to a school which is a long way from her village. But Bina finds the long walk to the school, anything but boring. For it is a walk across the mountains, the river and through the jungles—that surprises her with many fun-filled adventures. There is the sweet story of Rakesh and his cherry tree, and the story of Bisnu whose village is threatened by a man-eating panther. In this mix, there is also little Sunil whose Chachi dies one day at six in the evening and comes back to life exactly twenty minutes later.

It is only through these short stories that I can put down on paper the many characters in my head, for I enjoy nothing more than writing and keeping my readers entertained. And sitting here in a quaint hill station, there is nothing better to do than just that.

Ruskin Bond

# CHACHI'S FUNERAL

Chachi died at 6 p.m. on Wednesday, 5 April, and came to life again exactly twenty minutes later. This is how it happened.

Chachi was, as a rule, a fairly tolerant, easy-going person, who waddled about the house without paying much attention to the swarms of small sons, daughters, nephews and nieces who poured in and out of the rooms. But she had taken a particular aversion to her ten-year-old nephew, Sunil. She was a simple woman and could not understand Sunil. He was a little brighter than her own sons, more sensitive, and inclined to resent a scolding or a cuff across the head. He was better looking than her own children. All this, in addition to the fact that she resented having to cook for the boy while both his parents went out at office jobs, led her to grumble at him a little more than was really necessary.

Sunil sensed his aunt's jealousy and fanned its flames. He was a mischievous boy, and did little things to annoy her, like bursting paper-bags behind her while she dozed, or commenting on the width of her pyjamas when they were hung out to dry. On the evening of 5 April, he had been in particularly high spirits, and feeling hungry, entered the kitchen with the intention of helping himself to some honey. But the honey was on the top shelf, and Sunil wasn't quite tall enough to grasp the bottle. He got his fingers to it but as he tilted it towards him, it fell to the ground with a crash.

Chachi reached the scene of the accident before Sunil could slip away. Removing her slipper, she dealt him three or four furious blows across the head and shoulders. This done, she sat down on the floor and burst into tears.

Had the beating come from someone else, Sunil might have cried; but his pride was hurt, and instead of weeping, he muttered something under his breath and stormed out of the room.

Climbing the steps to the roof, he went to his secret hiding-place, a small hole in the wall of the unused barsati, where he kept his marbles, kite-string, tops, and a clasp-knife. Opening the knife, he plunged it thrice into the soft wood of the window-frame.

'I'll kill her!' he whispered fiercely, 'I'll kill her, I'll kill her!'

'Who are you going to kill, Sunil?'

It was his cousin Madhu, a dark slim girl of twelve, who aided and abetted him in most of his exploits. Sunil's Chachi was her 'Mammi'. It was a very big family.

'Chachi,' said Sunil. 'She hates me, I know. Well, I hate her too. This time I'll kill her.'

'How are you going to do it?'

'I'll stab with this.' He showed her the knife.

'Three times, in the heart.'

'But you'll be caught. The C.I.D. are very clever. Do you want to go to jail?'

'Won't they hang me?'

'They don't hang small boys. They send them to boarding-schools.'

'I don't want to go to a boarding-school.'

'Then better not kill your Chachi. At least not this way. I'll show you how.'

Madhu produced pencil and paper, went down on her hands and knees, and screwing up her face in sharp concentration, made a rough drawing of Chachi. Then, with a red crayon, she sketched in a big heart in the region of Chachi's stomach.

'Now,' she said, 'stab her to death!'

Sunil's eyes shone with excitement. Here was a great new game. You could always depend on Madhu for something original. He held the drawing against the woodwork, and plunged his knife three times into Chachi's pastel breast.

'You have killed her,' said Madhu.

'Is that all?'

'Well, if you like, we can cremate her.'

'All right.'

She took the torn paper, crumpled it up, produced a box of matches from Sunil's hiding-place, lit a match, and set fire to the paper. In a few minutes all that remained of Chachi were a few ashes.

'Poor Chachi,' said Madhu.

'Perhaps we shouldn't have done it,' said Sunil beginning to feel sorry.

'I know, we'll put her ashes in the river!'

'What river?'

'Oh, the drain will do.'

Madhu gathered the ashes together, and leant over the balcony of the roof. She threw out her arms, and the ashes drifted downwards.

Some of them settled on the pomegranate tree, a few reached the drain and were carried away by a sudden rush of kitchen-water. She turned to face Sunil.

Big tears were rolling down Sunil's cheeks.

'What are you crying for?' asked Madhu.

'Chachi. I didn't hate her so much.'

'Then why did you want to kill her?'

'Oh, that was different.'

'Come on, then, let's go down. I have to do my homework.'
As they came down the steps from the roof, Chachi emerged
from the kitchen.

'Oh Chachi!' shouted Sunil. He rushed to her and tried to
get his arms around her ample waist.

'Now what's up?' grumbled Chachi. 'What is it this time?'
'Nothing, Chachi. I love you so much. Please don't leave us.' A
look of suspicion crossed Chachi's face. She frowned down at
the boy. But she was reassured by the look of genuine affection
that she saw in his eyes.

'Perhaps he *does* care for me, after all,' she thought and
patting him gently on the head, she took him by the hand and
led him back to the kitchen.

# HIS NEIGHBOUR'S WIFE

No (said Arun, as we waited for dinner to be prepared), I did not fall in love with my neighbour's wife. It is not that kind of story.

Mind you, Leela was a most attractive woman. She was not beautiful or pretty; but she was handsome. Hers was the firm, athletic body of a sixteen-year-old boy, free of any surplus flesh. She bathed morning and evening, oiling herself well, so that her skin glowed a golden-brown in the winter sunshine. Her lips were often coloured with paan-juice, but her teeth were perfect.

I was her junior by about five years, and she called me her 'younger brother'. Her husband, who was forty to her thirty-two, was an official in the Customs and Excise Department: an extrovert, a hard-drinking, backslapping man, who spent a great deal of time on tour. Leela knew that he was not always faithful to her during these frequent absences; but she found solace in her own loyalty and in the well-being of her one child, a boy called Chandu.

I did not care for the boy. He had been well-spoilt, and took great delight in disturbing me whenever I was at work. He entered my rooms uninvited, knocked my books about, and, if guests were present, made insulting remarks about them to their faces.

Leela, during her lonely evenings, would often ask me to sit on her verandah and talk to her. The day's work done, she would relax with a hookah. Smoking a hookah was a habit she had brought with her from her village near Agra, and it was a habit she refused to give up. She liked to talk; and, as I was a good listener, she soon grew fond of me. The fact that I was twenty-six years old, and still a bachelor, never failed to astonish her.

It was not long before she took upon herself the responsibility for getting me married. I found it useless to protest. She did not believe me when I told her that I could not afford to marry, that I preferred a bachelor's life. A wife, she insisted, was an asset to any man. A wife reduced expenses. Where did I eat? At a hotel, of course. That must cost me at least sixty rupees a month, even on a vegetarian diet. But if I had a simple, homely wife to do the cooking, we could both eat well for less than that.

Leela fingered my shirt, observing that a button was missing and that the collar was frayed. She remarked on my pale face and general look of debility; and told me that I would fall victim to all kinds of diseases if I did not find someone to look after me. What I needed, she declared between puffs at the hookah, was a woman—a young, healthy, buxom woman, preferably from a village near Agra. 'If I could find someone like you,' I said slyly, 'I would not mind getting married.'

She appeared neither flattered nor offended by my remark.

'Don't marry an older woman,' she advised. 'Never take a wife who is more experienced in the ways of the world than you are. You just leave it to me, I'll find a suitable bride for you.'

To please Leela, I agreed to this arrangement, thinking she would not take it seriously. But, two days later, when she suggested that I accompany her to a certain distinguished home for orphan girls, I became alarmed. I refused to have anything to do with her project.

'Don't you have confidence in me?' she asked. 'You said you would like a girl who resembled me. I know one who looks just as I did ten years ago.'

'I like you as you are now,' I said. 'Not as you were ten years ago.'

'Of course. We shall arrange for you to see the girl first.'

'You don't understand,' I protested. 'It's not that I feel I have to be in love with someone before marrying her—I know you would choose a fine girl, and I would really prefer someone who is homely and simple to an M.A. with honours in psychology— it's just that I'm not ready for it. I want another year or two of freedom. I don't want to be chained down. To be frank, I don't want the responsibility.'

'A little responsibility will make a man of you,' said Leela; but she did not insist on my accompanying her to the orphanage, and the matter was allowed to rest for a few days.

I was beginning to hope that Leela had reconciled herself to allowing one man to remain single in a world full of husbands when, one morning, she accosted me on the verandah with an open newspaper, which she thrust in front of my nose.

'There!' she said triumphantly. 'What do you think of that? I did it to surprise you.'

She had certainly succeeded in surprising me. Her henna-stained forefinger rested on an advertisement in the matrimonial columns.

> Bachelor journalist, age 25, seeks attractive young wife
> well-versed in household duties. Caste, religion no bar.
> Dowry optional.

I must admit that Leela had made a good job of it. In a few

days the replies began to come in, usually from the parents of the girls concerned. Each applicant wanted to know how much money I was earning. At the same time, they took the trouble to list their own connections and the high positions occupied by relatives. Some parents enclosed their daughters' photographs. They were very good photographs, though there had been a certain amount of touching-up.

I studied the pictures with interest. Perhaps marriage wasn't such a bad proposition, after all. I selected the photographs of the three girls I most fancied and showed them to Leela.

To my surprise, she disapproved of all three. One of the girls she said, had a face like a hermaphrodite; another obviously suffered from tuberculosis; and the third was undoubtedly an adventuress. Leela decided that the whole idea of the advertisement had been a mistake. She was sorry she had inserted it; the only replies we were likely to get would be from fortune-hunters. And I had no fortune.

So we destroyed the letters. I tried to keep some of the photographs, but Leela tore them up too.

And so, for some time, there were no more attempts at getting me married.

Leela and I met nearly every day, but we spoke of other things. Sometimes, in the evenings, she would make me sit on the chawpoy opposite her, and then she would draw up her hookah and tell me stories about her village and her family. I was getting used to the boy, too, and even growing rather fond of him.

All this came to an end when Leela's husband went and got himself killed. He was shot by a bootlegger who had decided to get rid of the Excise man rather than pay him an exorbitant sum of money. It meant that Leela had to give up her quarters and return to her village near Agra. She waited until the boy's school-term had finished, and then she packed their things and bought two tickets, third-class to Agra.

Something, I could see, had been troubling her, and when I saw her off at the station I realized what it was. She was having a fit of conscience about my continued bachelorhood.

'In my village,' she said confidently, leaning out from the carriage window, 'there is a very comely young girl, a distant relative of mine, I shall speak to the parents.'

And then I said something which I had not considered before: which had never, until that moment, entered my head. And I was no less surprised than Leela when the words came tumbling out of my mouth: 'Why don't *you* marry me now?'

Arun didn't have time to finish his story because, just as this interesting stage, the dinner arrived.

But the dinner brought with it the end of his story.

It was served by his wife, a magnificent woman, strong and handsome, who could only have been Leela. And a few minutes later, Chandu, Arun's stepson, charged into the house, complaining that he was famished.

Arun introduced me to his wife, and we exchanged the usual formalities.

'But why hasn't your friend brought his family with him?' she asked.

'Family? Because he's still a bachelor!'

And then as he watched his wife's expression change from a look of mild indifference to one of deep concern, he hurriedly changed the subject.

# THE CHERRY TREE

One day, when Rakesh was six, he walked home from the Mussoorie bazaar eating cherries. They were a little sweet, a little sour; small, bright red cherries which had come all the way from the Kashmir Valley.

Here in the Himalayan foothills where Rakesh lived, there were not many fruit trees. The soil was stony, and the dry cold winds stunted the growth of most plants. But on the more sheltered slopes there were forests of oak and deodar.

Rakesh lived with his grandfather on the outskirts of Mussoorie, just where the forest began. His father and mother lived in a small village fifty miles away, where they grew maize and rice and barley in narrow terraced fields on the lower slopes of the mountain. But there were no schools in the village, and Rakesh's parents were keen that he should go to school. As soon as he was of school-going age, they sent him to stay with his grandfather in Mussoorie.

Grandfather was a retired forest ranger. He had a little cottage outside the town.

Rakesh was on his way home from school when he bought the cherries. He paid fifty paise for the bunch. It took him about half an hour to walk home, and by the time he reached the cottage there were only three cherries left.

'Have a cherry, Grandfather,' he said, as soon as he saw his grandfather in the garden.

Grandfather took one cherry and Rakesh promptly ate the other two. He kept the last seed in this mouth for some time, rolling it round and round on his tongue until all the tang had gone. Then he placed the seed on the palm of his hand and studied it.

'Are cherry seeds lucky?' asked Rakesh.

'Of course.'

'Then I'll keep it.'

'Nothing is lucky if you put it away. If you want luck, you must put it to some use.'

'What can I do with a seed?'

'Plant it.'

So Rakesh found a small shade and began to dig up a flower bed.

'Hey, not there,' said Grandfather. 'I've sown mustard in that bed. Plant it in that shady corner where it won't be disturbed.'

Rakesh went to a corner of the garden where the earth was soft and yielding. He did not have to dig. He pressed the seed into the soil with his thumb and it went right in.

Then he had his lunch and ran off to play cricket with his friends and forgot all about the cherry seed.

When it was winter in the hills, a cold wind blew down from the snows and went *wboo-wboo-wboo* through the deodar trees, and the garden was dry and bare. In the evenings, Grandfather told Rakesh stories—stories about people who turned into animals, and ghosts who lived in trees, and beans that jumped and stones that wept—and in turn Rakesh would read to him from the newspaper, Grandfather's eyesight being rather weak. Rakesh found the newspaper very dull—especially after the stories—but Grandfather wanted all the news…

They knew it was spring when the wild duck flew north again, to Siberia. Early in the morning, when he got up to chop wood and light a fire, Rakesh saw the V-shaped formation streaming northwards, the calls of the birds carrying clearly through the thin mountain air.

One morning in the garden, he bent to pick up what he thought was a small twig and found to his surprise that it was well rooted. He stared at it for a moment, then ran to fetch Grandfather, calling, 'Dada, come and look, the cherry tree has come up!'

'What cherry tree?' asked Grandfather, who had forgotten about it.

'The seed we planted last year—look, it's come up!'

Rakesh went down on his haunches, while Grandfather bent almost double and peered down at the tiny tree. It was about four inches high.

'Yes, it's a cherry tree,' said Grandfather. 'You should water it now and then.'

Rakesh ran indoors and came back with a bucket of water.

'Don't drown it!' said Grandfather.

Rakesh gave it a sprinkling and circled it with pebbles.

'What are the pebbles for?' asked Grandfather.

'For privacy,' said Rakesh.

He looked at the tree every morning but it did not seem to be growing very fast. So he stopped looking at it—except quickly, out of the corner of his eye. And, after a week or two, when he allowed himself to look at it properly, he found that it had grown—at least an inch!

That year the monsoon rains came early and Rakesh plodded to and from school in raincoat and gum boots. Ferns sprang from the trunks of trees, strange-looking lilies came up in the long grass, and even when it wasn't raining the trees dripped, and mist came curling up the valley. The cherry tree grew quickly in this season.

It was about two feet high when a goat entered the garden and ate all the leaves. Only the main stem and two thin branches remained.

'Never mind,' said Grandfather, seeing that Rakesh was upset. 'It will grow again, cherry trees are tough.'

Towards the end of the rainy season new leaves appeared on the tree. Then a woman cutting grass scrambled down the hillside, her scythe swishing through the heavy monsoon foliage. She did not try to avoid the tree: one sweep, and the cherry tree was cut in two.

When Grandfather saw what had happened, he went after the woman and scolded her; but the damage could not be repaired.

'Maybe it will die now,' said Rakesh.

'Maybe,' said Grandfather.

But the cherry tree had no intention of dying.

By the time summer came round again, it had sent out several new shoots with tender green leaves. Rakesh had grown taller too. He was eight now, a sturdy boy with curly black hair and deep black eyes. Blackberry eyes, Grandfather called them.

That monsoon Rakesh went home to his village, to help his father and mother with the planting and ploughing and sowing. He was thinner but stronger when he came back to Grandfather's house at the end of the rains, to find that the cherry tree had grown another foot. It was now up to his chest.

Even when there was rain, Rakesh would sometimes water the tree. He wanted it to know that he was there.

One day he found a bright green praying mantis perched on a branch, peering at him with bulging eyes. Rakesh let it remain there. It was the cherry tree's first visitor.

The next visitor was a hairy caterpillar, who started making a meal of the leaves. Rakesh removed it quickly and dropped it on a heap of dry leaves.

'They're pretty leaves,' said Rakesh. 'And they are always ready to dance. If there's a breeze.'

After Grandfather had come indoors, Rakesh went into the garden and lay down on the grass beneath the tree. He gazed up through the leaves at the great blue sky; and turning on his side, he could see the mountain striding away into the clouds. He was still lying beneath the tree when the evening shadows crept across the garden. Grandfather came back and sat down beside Rakesh, and they waited in silence until the stars came out and the nightjar began to call. In the forest below, the crickets and cicadas began tuning up; and suddenly the tree was full of the sound of insects.

'There are so many trees in the forest,' said Rakesh. 'What's so special about this tree? Why do we like it so much?'

'We planted it ourselves,' said Grandfather. 'That's why it's special.'

'Just one small seed,' said Rakesh, and he touched the smooth bark of the tree that had grown. He ran his hand along the trunk of the tree and put his finger to the tip of a leaf. 'I wonder,' he whispered, 'is this what it feels to be God?'

# PANTHER'S MOON

I

In the entire village, he was the first to get up. Even the dog, a big hill mastiff called Sheroo, was asleep in a corner of the dark room, curled up near the cold embers of the previous night's fire. Bisnu's tousled head emerged from his blanket. He rubbed the sleep from his eyes and sat up on his haunches. Then, gathering his wits, he crawled in the direction of the loud ticking that came from the battered little clock which occupied the second most honoured place in a niche in the wall. The most honoured place belonged to a picture of Ganesha, the god of learning, who had an elephant's head and a fat boy's body.

Bringing his face close to the clock, Bisnu could just make out the hands. It was five o'clock. He had half an hour in which to get ready and leave.

He got up, in vest and underpants, and moved quietly towards the door. The soft tread of his bare feet woke Sheroo, and the big black dog rose silently and padded behind the boy. The door opened and closed, and then the boy and the dog were outside in the early dawn. The month was June, and the nights were warm, even in the Himalayan valleys; but there was fresh dew on the grass. Bisnu felt the dew beneath his feet.

He took a deep breath and began walking down to the stream.

The sound of the stream filled the small valley. At that early hour of the morning, it was the only sound; but Bisnu was hardly conscious of it. It was a sound he lived with and took for granted. It was only when he had crossed the hill, on his way to the town—and the sound of the stream grew distant—that he really began to notice it. And it was only when the stream was too far away to be heard that he really missed its sound.

He slipped out of his underclothes, gazed for a few moments at the goose pimples rising on his flesh, and then dashed into the shallow stream. As he went further in, the cold mountain water reached his loins and navel, and he gasped with shock and pleasure. He drifted slowly with the current, swam across to a small inlet which formed a fairly deep pool, and plunged into the water. Sheroo hated cold water at this early hour. Had the sun been up, he would not have hesitated to join Bisnu. Now he contented himself with sitting on a smooth rock and gazing placidly at the slim brown boy splashing about in the clear water, in the widening light of dawn.

Bisnu did not stay long in the water. There wasn't time. When he returned to the house, he found his mother up, making tea and chapattis. His sister, Puja, was still asleep. She was a little older than Bisnu, a pretty girl with large black eyes, good teeth and strong arms and legs. During the day, she helped her mother in the house and in the fields. She did not go to the school with Bisnu. But when he came home in the evenings, he would try teaching her some of the things he had learnt. Their father was dead. Bisnu, at twelve, considered himself the head of the family.

He ate two chapattis, after spreading butter-oil on them. He drank a glass of hot sweet tea. His mother gave two thick chapattis to Sheroo, and the dog wolfed them down in a few minutes. Then she wrapped two chapattis and a gourd curry in some big green leaves, and handed these to Bisnu. This was his lunch packet. His mother and Puja would take their meal afterwards.

When Bisnu was dressed, he stood with folded hands before the picture of Ganesha. Ganesha is the god who blesses all beginnings. The author who begins to write a new book, the banker who opens a new ledger, the traveller who starts on a journey, all invoke the kindly help of Ganesha. And as Bisnu made a journey every day, he never left without the goodwill of the elephant-headed god.

How, one might ask, did Ganesha get his elephant's head?

When born, he was a beautiful child. Parvati, his mother, was so proud of him that she went about showing him to everyone. Unfortunately she made the mistake of showing the child to that envious planet, Saturn, who promptly burnt off poor Ganesha's head. Parvati in despair went to Brahma, the Creator, for a new head for her son. He had no head to give her, but advised her to search for some man or animal caught in a sinful or wrong act. Parvati wandered about until she came upon an elephant sleeping with its head the wrong way, that is, to the south. She promptly removed the elephant's head and planted it on Ganesha's shoulders, where it took root.

Bisnu knew this story. He had heard it from his mother.

Wearing a white shirt and black shorts, and a pair of worn white keds, he was ready for his long walk to school, five miles up the mountain.

His sister woke up just as he was about to leave. She pushed the hair away from her face and gave Bisnu one of her rare smiles.

'I hope you have not forgotten,' she said.

'Forgotten?' said Bisnu, pretending innocence. 'Is there

anything I am supposed to remember?'

'Don't tease me. You promised to buy me a pair of bangles, remember? I hope you won't spend the money on sweets, as you did last time.'

'Oh, yes, your bangles,' said Bisnu. 'Girls have nothing better to do than waste money on trinkets. Now, don't lose your temper! I'll get them for you. Red and gold are the colours you want?'

'Yes, Brother,' said Puja gently, pleased that Bisnu had remembered the colours. 'And for your dinner tonight we'll make you something special. Won't we, Mother?'

'Yes. But hurry up and dress. There is some ploughing to be done today. The rains will soon be here, if the gods are kind.'

'The monsoon will be late this year,' said Bisnu. 'Mr Nautiyal, our teacher, told us so. He said it had nothing to do with the gods.'

'Be off, you are getting late,' said Puja, before Bisnu could begin an argument with his mother. She was diligently winding the old clock. It was quite light in the room. The sun would be up any minute.

Bisnu shouldered his school bag, kissed his mother, pinched his sister's cheeks and left the house. He started climbing the steep path up the mountainside. Sheroo bounded ahead; for he, too, always went with Bisnu to school.

Five miles to school. Every day, except Sunday, Bisnu walked five miles to school; and in the evening, he walked home again. There was no school in his own small village of Manjari, for the village consisted of only five families. The nearest school was at Kemptee, a small township on the bus route through the district of Garhwal. A number of boys walked to school, from distances of two or three miles; their villages were not quite as remote as Manjari. But Bisnu's village lay right at the bottom of the mountain, a drop of over two thousand feet from Kemptee. There was no proper road between the village and the town.

In Kemptee there was a school, a small mission hospital, a post office and several shops. In Manjari village there were none of these amenities. If you were sick, you stayed at home until you got well; if you were very sick, you walked or were carried to the hospital, up the five mile path. If you wanted to buy something, you went without it; but if you wanted it very badly, you could walk the five miles to Kemptee.

Manjari was known as the Five Mile Village.

Twice a week, if there were any letters, a postman came to the village. Bisnu usually passed the postman on his way to and from school.

There were other boys in Manjari village, but Bisnu was the only one who went to school. His mother would not have fussed if he had stayed at home and worked in the fields. That was what the other boys did; all except lazy Chittru, who preferred fishing in the stream or helping himself to the fruit of other people's trees. But Bisnu went to school. He went because he wanted to. No one could force him to go; and no one could stop him from going. He had set his heart on receiving a good schooling. He wanted to read and write as well as anyone in the big world, the world that seemed to begin only where the mountains ended. He felt cut off from the world in his small valley. He would rather live at the top of a mountain than at the bottom of one. That was why he liked climbing to Kemptee, it took him to the top of the mountain; and from its ridge he could look down on his own valley to the north, and on the wide endless plains stretching towards the south.

The plainsman looks to the hills for the needs of his spirit but the hill man looks to the plains for a living.

Leaving the village and the fields below him, Bisnu climbed steadily up the bare hillside, now dry and brown. By the time the sun was up, he had entered the welcome shade of an oak and rhododendron forest. Sheroo went bounding ahead, chasing squirrels and barking at langoors.

A colony of langoors lived in the oak forest. They fed on oak leaves, acorns and other green things, and usually remained in the trees, coming down to the ground only to play or bask in the sun. They were beautiful, supple-limbed animals, with black faces and silver-grey coats and long, sensitive tails. They leapt from tree to tree with great agility. The young ones wrestled on the grass like boys.

A dignified community, the langoors did not have the cheekiness or dishonest habits of the red monkeys of the plains; they did not approach dogs or humans. But they had grown used to Bisnu's comings and goings, and did not fear him. Some of the older ones would watch him quietly, a little puzzled. They did not go near the town, because the Kemptee boys threw stones at them. And anyway, the oak forest gave them all the food they required.

Emerging from the trees, Bisnu crossed a small brook. Here he stopped to drink the fresh clean water of a spring. The brook tumbled down the mountain and joined the river a little below Bisnu's village. Coming from another direction was a second path, and at the junction of the two paths Sarru was waiting for him.

Sarru came from a small village about three miles from Bisnu's and closer to the town. He had two large milk cans slung over his shoulders. Every morning he carried this milk to town, selling one can to the school and the other to Mrs Taylor, the lady doctor at the small mission hospital. He was a little older than Bisnu but not as well-built.

They hailed each other, and Sarru fell into step beside Bisnu. They often met at this spot, keeping each other company for the remaining two miles to Kemptee.

'There was a panther in our village last night,' said Sarru.

This information interested but did not excite Bisnu. Panthers were common enough in the hills and did not usually present a problem except during the winter months, when their natural prey was scarce. Then, occasionally, a panther would take to haunting the outskirts of a village, seizing a careless dog or a stray goat.

'Did you lose any animals?' asked Bisnu.

'No. It tried to get into the cowshed but the dogs set up an alarm. We drove it off.'

'It must be the same one which came around last winter. We lost a calf and two dogs in our village.'

'Wasn't that the one the shikaris wounded? I hope it hasn't become a cattle lifter.'

'It could be the same. It has a bullet in its leg. These hunters are the people who cause all the trouble. They think it's easy to shoot a panther. It would be better if they missed altogether, but they usually wound it.'

'And then the panther's too slow to catch the barking deer, and starts on our own animals.'

'We're lucky it didn't become a man-eater. Do you remember the man-eater six years ago? I was very small then. My father told me all about it. Ten people were killed in our valley alone. What happened to it?'

'I don't know. Some say it poisoned itself when it ate the headman of another village.'

Bisnu laughed. 'No one liked that old villain. He must have been a man-eater himself in some previous existence!' They linked arms and scrambled up the stony path. Sheroo began barking and ran ahead. Someone was coming down the path.

It was Mela Ram, the postman.

## II

'Any letters for us?' asked Bisnu and Sarru together.

They never received any letters but that did not stop them from asking. It was one way of finding out who had received letters.

'You're welcome to all of them,' said Mela Ram, 'if you'll carry my bag for me.'

'Not today,' said Sarru. 'We're busy today. Is there a letter from Corporal Ghanshyam for his family?'

'Yes, there is a postcard for his people. He is posted on the Ladakh border now and finds it very cold there.'

Postcards, unlike sealed letters, were considered public property and were read by everyone. The senders knew that too, and so Corporal Ghanshyam Singh was careful to mention that he expected a promotion very soon. He wanted everyone in his village to know it.

Mela Ram, complaining of sore feet, continued on his way, and the boys carried on up the path. It was eight o'clock when they reached Kemptee. Dr Taylor's outpatients were just beginning to trickle in at the hospital gate. The doctor was trying to prop up a rose creeper which had blown down during the night. She liked attending to her plants in the mornings, before starting on her patients. She found this helped her in her work. There was a lot in common between ailing plants and ailing people.

Dr Taylor was fifty, white-haired but fresh in the face and full of vitality. She had been in India for twenty years, and ten of these had been spent working in the hill regions.

She saw Bisnu coming down the road. She knew about

the boy and his long walk to school and admired him for his keenness and sense of purpose. She wished there were more like him.

Bisnu greeted her shyly. Sheroo barked and put his paws up on the gate.

'Yes, there's a bone for you,' said Dr Taylor. She often put aside bones for the big black dog, for she knew that Bisnu's people could not afford to give the dog a regular diet of meat—though he did well enough on milk and chapattis.

She threw the bone over the gate and Sheroo caught it before it fell. The school bell began ringing and Bisnu broke into a run. Sheroo loped along behind the boy.

When Bisnu entered the school gate, Sheroo sat down on the grass of the compound. He would remain there until the lunchbreak. He knew of various ways of amusing himself during school hours and had friends among the bazaar dogs. But just then he didn't want company. He had his bone to get on with.

Mr Nautiyal, Bisnu's teacher, was in a bad mood. He was a keen rose grower and only that morning, on getting up and looking out of his bedroom window, he had been horrified to see a herd of goats in his garden. He had chased them down the road with a stick but the damage had already been done. His prize roses had all been consumed.

Mr Nautiyal had been so upset that he had gone without his breakfast. He had also cut himself whilst shaving. Thus, his mood had gone from bad to worse. Several times during the day, he brought down his ruler on the knuckles of any boy who irritated him. Bisnu was one of his best pupils. But even Bisnu irritated him by asking too many questions about a new sum which Mr Nautiyal didn't feel like explaining.

That was the kind of day it was for Mr Nautiyal. Most schoolteachers know similar days.

'Poor Mr Nautiyal,' thought Bisnu. 'I wonder why he's so upset. It must be because of his pay. He doesn't get much money. But he's a good teacher. I hope he doesn't take another job.'

But after Mr Nautiyal had eaten his lunch, his mood improved (as it always did after a meal), and the rest of the day passed serenely. Armed with a bundle of homework, Bisnu came out from the school compound at four o'clock, and was immediately joined by Sheroo. He proceeded down the road in the company of several of his classfellows. But he did not linger long in the bazaar. There were five miles to walk, and he did not like to get home too late. Usually, he reached his house just as it was beginning to get dark. Sarru had gone home long ago, and Bisnu had to make the return journey on his own. It was a good opportunity to memorize the words of an English poem he had been asked to learn.

Bisnu had reached the little brook when he remembered the bangles he had promised to buy for his sister.

'Oh, I've forgotten them again,' he said aloud. 'Now I'll catch it—and she's probably made something special for my dinner!'

Sheroo, to whom these words were addressed, paid no attention but bounded off into the oak forest. Bisnu looked around for the monkeys but they were nowhere to be seen.

'Strange,' he thought, 'I wonder why they have disappeared.' He was startled by a sudden sharp cry, followed by a fierce yelp. He knew at once that Sheroo was in trouble. The noise came from the bushes down the khud, into which the dog had rushed but a few seconds previously.

Bisnu jumped off the path and ran down the slope towards the bushes. There was no dog and not a sound. He whistled and called, but there was no response. Then he saw something lying on the dry grass. He picked it up. It was a portion of a dog's collar, stained with blood. It was Sheroo's collar and

Sheroo's blood.

Bisnu did not search further. He knew, without a doubt, that Sheroo had been seized by a panther. No other animal could have attacked so silently and swiftly and carried off a big dog without a struggle. Sheroo was dead—must have been dead within seconds of being caught and flung into the air. Bisnu knew the danger that lay in wait for him if he followed the blood trail through the trees. The panther would attack anyone who interfered with its meal. With tears starting in his eyes, Bisnu carried on down the path to the village. His fingers still clutched the little bit of bloodstained collar that was all that was left to him of his dog.

III

Bisnu was not a very sentimental boy, but he sorrowed for his dog who had been his companion on many a hike into the hills and forests. He did not sleep that night, but turned restlessly from side to side moaning softly. After some time he felt Puja's hand on his head. She began stroking his brow. He took her hand in his own and the clasp of her rough, warm familiar hand gave him a feeling of comfort and security.

Next morning, when he went down to the stream to bathe, he missed the presence of his dog. He did not stay long in the water. It wasn't as much fun when there was no Sheroo to watch him.

When Bisnu's mother gave him his food, she told him to be careful and hurry home that evening. A panther, even if it is only a cowardly lifter of sheep or dogs, is not to be trifled with. And this particular panther had shown some daring by seizing the dog even before it was dark.

Still, there was no question of staying away from school. If Bisnu remained at home every time a panther put in an appearance, he might just as well stop going to school altogether.

He set off even earlier than usual and reached the meeting of the paths long before Sarru. He did not wait for his friend, because he did not feel like talking about the loss of his dog. It was not the day for the postman, and so Bisnu reached Kemptee without meeting anyone on the way. He tried creeping past the hospital gate unnoticed, but Dr Taylor saw him and the first thing she said was: 'Where's Sheroo? I've got something for him.'

When Dr Taylor saw the boy's face, she knew at once that something was wrong.

'What is it, Bisnu?' she asked. She looked quickly up and down the road. 'Is it Sheroo?'

He nodded gravely.

'A panther took him,' he said.

'In the village?'

'No, while we were walking home through the forest. I did not see anything—but I heard.'

Dr Taylor knew that there was nothing she could say that would console him, and she tried to conceal the bone which she had brought out for the dog, but Bisnu noticed her hiding it behind her back and the tears welled up in his eyes. He turned away and began running down the road.

His schoolfellows noticed Sheroo's absence and questioned Bisnu. He had to tell them everything. They were full of sympathy, but they were also quite thrilled at what had happened and kept pestering Bisnu for all the details. There was a lot of noise in the classroom, and Mr Nautiyal had to call for order. When he learnt what had happened, he patted Bisnu on the head and told him that he need not attend school for the rest of the day. But Bisnu did not want to go home. After school, he got into a fight with one of the boys, and that helped him forget.

IV

The panther that plunged the village into an atmosphere of gloom and terror may not have been the same panther that took Sheroo. There was no way of knowing, and it would have made no difference, because the panther that came by night and struck at the people of Manjari was that most feared of wild creatures, a man-eater.

Nine-year-old Sanjay, son of Kalam Singh, was the first child to be attacked by the panther.

Kalam Singh's house was the last in the village and nearest the stream. Like the other houses, it was quite small, just a room above and a stable below, with steps leading up from outside the house. He lived there with his wife, two sons (Sanjay was the youngest) and little daughter Basanti who had just turned three.

Sanjay had brought his father's cows home after grazing them on the hillside in the company of other children. He had also brought home an edible wild plant, which his mother cooked into a tasty dish for their evening meal. They had their food at dusk, sitting on the floor of their single room, and soon after settled down for the night. Sanjay curled up in his favourite spot, with his head near the door, where he got a little fresh air. As the nights were warm, the door was usually left a little ajar. Sanjay's mother piled ash on the embers of the fire and the family was soon asleep.

No one heard the stealthy padding of a panther approaching the door, pushing it wide open. But suddenly there were sounds of a frantic struggle, and Sanjay's stifled cries were mixed with the grunts of the panther. Kalam Singh leapt to his feet with a shout. The panther had dragged Sanjay out of the door and was pulling him down the steps, when Kalam Singh started battering at the animal with a large stone. The rest of the family screamed in terror, rousing the entire village. A number of men came to Kalam Singh's assistance, and the panther was driven off. But Sanjay lay unconscious.

Someone brought a lantern and the boy's mother screamed when she saw her small son with his head lying in a pool of blood. It looked as if the side of his head had been eaten off by the panther. But he was still alive, and as Kalam Singh plastered ash on the boy's head to stop the bleeding, he found that though the scalp had been torn off one side of the head, the bare bone was smooth and unbroken.

'He won't live through the night,' said a neighbour. 'We'll have to carry him down to the river in the morning.'

The dead were always cremated on the banks of a small river which flowed past Manjari village.

Suddenly the panther, still prowling about the village, called out in rage and frustration, and the villagers rushed to their homes in panic and barricaded themselves in for the night.

Sanjay's mother sat by the boy for the rest of the night, weeping and watching. Towards dawn he started to moan and show signs of coming round. At this sign of returning consciousness, Kalam Singh rose determinedly and looked around for his stick.

He told his elder son to remain behind with the mother and daughter, as he was going to take Sanjay to Dr Taylor at the hospital.

'See, he is moaning and in pain,' said Kalam Singh. 'That means he has a chance to live if he can be treated at once.'

With a stout stick in his hand, and Sanjay on his back, Kalam Singh set off on the two miles of hard mountain track to the hospital at Kemptee. His son, a bloodstained cloth around his head, was moaning but still unconscious. When at last Kalam Singh climbed up through the last fields below the hospital, he asked for the doctor and stammered out an account of what had happened.

It was a terrible injury, as Dr Taylor discovered. The bone over almost one-third of the head was bare and the scalp was torn all round. As the father told his story, the doctor cleaned and dressed the wound, and then gave Sanjay a shot of penicillin to prevent sepsis. Later, Kalam Singh carried the boy home again.

V

After this, the panther went away for some time. But the people of Manjari could not be sure of its whereabouts. They kept to their houses after dark and shut their doors. Bisnu had to stop going to school, because there was no one to accompany him and it was dangerous to go alone. This worried him, because his final exam was only a few weeks off and he would be missing important classwork. When he wasn't in the fields, helping with the sowing of rice and maize, he would be sitting in the shade of a chestnut tree, going through his well-thumbed second-hand school books. He had no other reading, except for a copy of the Ramayana and a Hindi translation of *Alice's Adventures in Wonderland*. These were well-preserved, read only in fits and starts, and usually kept locked in his mother's old tin trunk.

Sanjay had nightmares for several nights and woke up screaming. But with the resilience of youth, he quickly recovered. At the end of the week he was able to walk to the hospital, though his father always accompanied him. Even a desperate panther will hesitate to attack a party of two. Sanjay, with his thin little face and huge bandaged head, looked a pathetic figure, but he was getting better and the wound looked healthy.

Bisnu often went to see him, and the two boys spent long hours together near the stream. Sometimes Chittru would join them, and they would try catching fish with a home-made net.

They were often successful in taking home one or two mountain trout. Sometimes, Bisnu and Chittru wrestled in the shallow water or on the grassy banks of the stream. Chittru was a chubby boy with a broad chest, strong legs and thighs, and when he used his weight he got Bisnu under him. But Bisnu was hard and wiry and had very strong wrists and fingers. When he had Chittru in a vice, the bigger boy would cry out and give up the struggle. Sanjay could not join in these games.

He had never been a very strong boy and he needed plenty of rest if his wounds were to heal well.

The panther had not been seen for over a week, and the people of Manjari were beginning to hope that it might have moved on over the mountain or further down the valley.

'I think I can start going to school again,' said Bisnu. 'The panther has gone away.'

'Don't be too sure,' said Puja. 'The moon is full these days and perhaps it is only being cautious.'

'Wait a few days,' said their mother. 'It is better to wait. Perhaps you could go the day after tomorrow when Sanjay goes to the hospital with his father. Then you will not be alone.'

And so, two days later, Bisnu went up to Kemptee with Sanjay and Kalam Singh. Sanjay's wound had almost healed over. Little islets of flesh had grown over the bone. Dr Taylor told him that he need come to see her only once a fortnight, instead of every third day.

Bisnu went to his school, and was given a warm welcome by his friends and by Mr Nautiyal.

'You'll have to work hard,' said his teacher. 'You have to catch up with the others. If you like, I can give you some extra time after classes.'

'Thank you, sir, but it will make me late,' said Bisnu. 'I must get home before it is dark, otherwise my mother will worry. I think the panther has gone but nothing is certain.'

'Well, you mustn't take risks. Do your best, Bisnu. Work hard and you'll soon catch up with your lessons.'

Sanjay and Kalam Singh were waiting for him outside the school. Together they took the path down to Manjari, passing the postman on the way. Mela Ram said he had heard that the panther was in another district and that there was nothing to fear. He was on his rounds again.

Nothing happened on the way. The langoors were back in their favourite part of the forest. Bisnu got home just as the kerosene lamp was being lit. Puja met him at the door with a winsome smile.

'Did you get the bangles?' she asked.

But Bisnu had forgotten again.

## VI

There had been a thunderstorm and some rain—a short, sharp shower which gave the villagers hope that the monsoon would arrive on time. It brought out the thunder lilies—pink, crocus-like flowers which sprang up on the hillsides immediately after a summer shower.

Bisnu, on his way home from school, was caught in the rain. He knew the shower would not last, so he took shelter in a small cave and, to pass the time, began doing sums, scratching figures in the damp earth with the end of a stick.

When the rain stopped, he came out from the cave and continued down the path. He wasn't in a hurry. The rain had made everything smell fresh and good. The scent from fallen pine needles rose from wet earth. The leaves of the oak trees had been washed clean and a light breeze turned them about, showing their silver undersides. The birds, refreshed and high-spirited, set up a terrific noise. The worst offenders were the yellow-bottomed bulbuls who squabbled and fought in the blackberry bushes. A barbet, high up in the branches of a deodar, set up its querulous, plaintive call. And a flock of bright green parrots came swooping down the hill to settle in a wild plum tree and feast on the unripe fruit. The langoors, too, had been revived by the rain. They leapt friskily from tree to tree greeting Bisnu with little grunts.

He was almost out of the oak forest when he heard a faint bleating. Presently, a little goat came stumbling up the path towards him. The kid was far from home and must have strayed from the rest of the herd. But it was not yet conscious of being lost. It came to Bisnu with a hop, skip and a jump and started nuzzling against his legs like a cat.

'I wonder who you belong to,' mused Bisnu, stroking the little creature. 'You'd better come home with me until someone claims you.'

He didn't have to take the kid in his arms. It was used to humans and followed close at his heels. Now that darkness was coming on, Bisnu walked a little faster.

He had not gone very far when he heard the sawing grunt of a panther.

The sound came from the hill to the right, and Bisnu judged the distance to be anything from 100 to 200 yards. He hesitated on the path, wondering what to do. Then he picked the kid up in his arms and hurried on in the direction of home and safety.

The panther called again, much closer now. If it was an ordinary panther, it would go away on finding that the kid was with Bisnu. If it was the man-eater, it would not hesitate to attack the boy, for no man-eater fears a human. There was no time to lose and there did not seem much point in running. Bisnu looked up and down the hillside. The forest was far behind him and there were only a few trees in his vicinity. He chose a spruce.

The branches of the Himalayan spruce are very brittle and snap easily beneath a heavy weight. They were strong enough to support Bisnu's light frame. It was unlikely they would take the weight of a full-grown panther. At least that was what Bisnu hoped.

Holding the kid with one arm, Bisnu gripped a low branch and swung himself up into the tree. He was a good climber. Slowly but confidently he climbed halfway up the tree, until he was about twelve feet above the ground. He couldn't go any higher without risking a fall.

He had barely settled himself in the crook of a branch when the panther came into the open, running into the clearing at a brisk trot. This was no stealthy approach, no wary stalking of its prey. It was the man-eater, all right. Bisnu felt a cold shiver run down his spine. He felt a little sick.

The panther stood in the clearing with a slight thrusting forward of the head. This gave it the appearance of gazing intently and rather short-sightedly at some invisible object in the clearing. But there is nothing short-sighted about a panther's vision. Its sight and hearing are acute.

Bisnu remained motionless in the tree and sent up a prayer to all the gods he could think of. But the kid began bleating. The panther looked up and gave its deep-throated, rasping grunt—a fearsome sound, calculated to strike terror in any treeborne animal. Many a monkey, petrified by a panther's roar, has fallen from its perch to make a meal for Mr Spots. The man-eater was trying the same technique on Bisnu. But though the boy was trembling with fright, he clung firmly to the base of the spruce tree.

The panther did not make any attempt to leap into the tree. Perhaps, it knew instinctively that this was not the type of tree that it could climb. Instead, it described a semicircle round the tree, keeping its face turned towards Bisnu. Then it disappeared into the bushes.

The man-eater was cunning. It hoped to put the boy off his guard, perhaps entice him down from the tree. For, a few seconds later, with a half-humorous growl, it rushed back into the clearing and then stopped, staring up at the boy in some surprise. The panther was getting frustrated. It snarled, and putting its forefeet up against the tree trunk began scratching at the bark in the manner of an ordinary domestic cat. The tree shook at each thud of the beast's paw.

Bisnu began shouting for help.

The moon had not yet come up. Down in Manjari village, Bisnu's mother and sister stood in their lighted doorway, gazing anxiously up the pathway. Every now and then, Puja would turn to take a look at the small clock.

Sanjay's father appeared in a field below. He had a kerosene lantern in his hand.

'Sister, isn't your boy home as yet?' he asked.

'No, he hasn't arrived. We are very worried. He should have been home an hour ago. Do you think the panther will be about tonight? There's going to be a moon.'

'True, but it will be dark for another hour. I will fetch the other menfolk, and we will go up the mountain for your boy. There may have been a landslide during the rain. Perhaps the path has been washed away.'

'Thank you, brother. But arm yourselves, just in case the panther is about.'

'I will take my spear,' said Kalam Singh. 'I have sworn to spear that devil when I find him. There is some evil spirit dwelling in the beast and it must be destroyed!'

'I am coming with you,' said Puja.

'No, you cannot go,' said her mother. 'It's bad enough that Bisnu is in danger. You stay at home with me. This is work for men.'

'I shall be safe with them,' insisted Puja. 'I am going, Mother!' And she jumped down the embankment into the field and followed Sanjay's father through the village.

Ten minutes later, two men armed with axes had joined Kalam Singh in the courtyard of his house, and the small party moved silently and swiftly up the mountain path. Puja walked in the middle of the group, holding the lantern. As soon as the village lights were hidden by a shoulder of the hill, the men began to shout—both to frighten the panther, if it was about, and to give themselves courage.

Bisnu's mother closed the front door and turned to the image of Ganesha, the god for comfort and help.

Bisnu's calls were carried on the wind, and Puja and the men heard him while they were still half a mile away. Their own shouts increased in volume and, hearing their voices, Bisnu felt strength return to his shaking limbs. Emboldened by the approach of his own people, he began shouting insults at the snarling panther, then throwing twigs and small branches at the enraged animal. The kid added its bleats to the boy's shouts, the birds took up the chorus. The langoors squealed and grunted, the searchers shouted themselves hoarse, and the panther howled with rage. The forest had never before been so noisy.

As the search party drew near, they could hear the panther's savage snarls, and hurried, fearing that perhaps Bisnu had been seized. Puja began to run.

'Don't rush ahead, girl,' said Kalam Singh. 'Stay between us.'

The panther, now aware of the approaching humans, stood still in the middle of the clearing, head thrust forward in a familiar stance. There seemed too many men for one panther.

When the animal saw the light of the lantern dancing between the trees, it turned, snarled defiance and hate, and without another look at the boy in the tree, disappeared into the bushes. It was not yet ready for a showdown.

VII

Nobody turned up to claim the little goat, so Bisnu kept it. A goat was a poor substitute for a dog, but, like Mary's lamb, it followed Bisnu wherever he went, and the boy couldn't help being touched by its devotion. He took it down to the stream, where it would skip about in the shallows and nibble the sweet grass that grew on the banks.

As for the panther, frustrated in its attempt on Bisnu's life, it did not wait long before attacking another human.

It was Chittru who came running down the path one afternoon, bubbling excitedly about the panther and the postman.

Chittru, deeming it safe to gather ripe bilberries in the daytime, had walked about half a mile up the path from the village, when he had stumbled across Mela Ram's mailbag lying on the ground. Of the postman himself there was no sign. But a trail of blood led through the bushes.

Once again, a party of men headed by Kalam Singh and accompanied by Bisnu and Chittru, went out to look for the postman. But though they found Mela Ram's bloodstained clothes, they could not find his body. The panther had made no mistake this time.

It was to be several weeks before Manjari had a new postman.

A few days after Mela Ram's disappearance, an old woman was sleeping with her head near the open door of her house. She had been advised to sleep inside with the door closed, but the nights were hot and anyway the old woman was a little deaf, and in the middle of the night, an hour before moonrise, the panther seized her by the throat. Her strangled cry woke her grown-up son, and all the men in the village woke up at his shouts and came running.

The panther dragged the old woman out of the house and down the steps, but left her when the men approached with their axes and spears, and made off into the bushes. The old woman was still alive, and the men made a rough stretcher of bamboo and vines and started carrying her up the path. But they had not gone far when she began to cough, and because of her terrible throat wounds, her lungs collapsed and she died.

It was the 'dark of the month'—the week of the new moon when nights are darkest.

Bisnu, closing the front door and lighting the kerosene lantern, said, 'I wonder where that panther is tonight!'

The panther was busy in another village: Sarru's village.

A woman and her daughter had been out in the evening bedding the cattle down in the stable. The girl had gone into the house and the woman was following. As she bent down to go in at the low door, the panther sprang from the bushes. Fortunately, one of its paws hit the doorpost and broke the force of the attack, or the woman would have been killed. When she cried out, the men came round shouting and the panther slunk off. The woman had deep scratches on her back and was badly shocked.

The next day, a small party of villagers presented themselves in front of the magistrate's office at Kemptee and demanded that something be done about the panther. But the magistrate was away on tour, and there was no one else in Kemptee who had a gun. Mr Nautiyal met the villagers and promised to write to a well-known shikari, but said that it would be at least a fortnight before the shikari would be able to come.

Bisnu was fretting because he could not go to school. Most boys would be only too happy to miss school, but when you are living in a remote village in the mountains and having an education is the only way of seeing the world, you look forward to going to school, even if it is five miles from home. Bisnu's exams were only two weeks off, and he didn't want to remain in the same class while the others were promoted. Besides, he knew he could pass even though he had missed a number of lessons. But he had to sit for the exams. He couldn't miss them.

'Cheer up, Bhaiya,' said Puja, as they sat drinking glasses of hot tea after their evening meal. 'The panther may go away once the rains break.'

'Even the rains are late this year,' said Bisnu. 'It's so hot and dry. Can't we open the door?'

'And be dragged down the steps by the panther?' said his mother. 'It isn't safe to have the window open, let alone the door.' And she went to the small window—through which a cat would have found difficulty in passing—and bolted it firmly.

With a sigh of resignation, Bisnu threw off all his clothes except his underwear and stretched himself out on the earthen floor.

'We will be rid of the beast soon,' said his mother. 'I know it in my heart. Our prayers will be heard, and you shall go to school and pass your exams.'

To cheer up her children, she told them a humorous story which had been handed down to her by her grandmother. It was all about a tiger, a panther and a bear, the three of whom were made to feel very foolish by a thief hiding in the hollow trunk of a banyan tree. Bisnu was sleepy and did not listen very attentively. He dropped off to sleep before the story was finished.

When he woke, it was dark and his mother and sister were

asleep on the cot. He wondered what it was that had woken him. He could hear his sister's easy breathing and the steady ticking of the clock. Far away an owl hooted—an unlucky sign, his mother would have said; but she was asleep and Bisnu was not superstitious.

And then he heard something scratching at the door, and the hair on his head felt tight and prickly. It was like a cat scratching, only louder. The door creaked a little whenever it felt the impact of the paw—a heavy paw, as Bisnu could tell from the dull sound it made.

'It's the panther,' he muttered under his breath, sitting up on the hard floor.

The door, he felt, was strong enough to resist the panther's weight. And if he set up an alarm, he could rouse the village. But the middle of the night was no time for the bravest of men to tackle a panther.

In a corner of the room stood a long bamboo stick with a sharp knife tied to one end, which Bisnu sometimes used for spearing fish. Crawling on all fours across the room, he grasped the home-made spear, and then scrambling on to a cupboard, he drew level with the skylight window. He could get his head and shoulders through the window.

'What are you doing up there?' said Puja, who had woken up at the sound of Bisnu shuffling about the room.

'Be quiet,' said Bisnu. 'You'll wake Mother.'

Their mother was awake by now. 'Come down from there, Bisnu. I can hear a noise outside.'

'Don't worry,' said Bisnu, who found himself looking down on the wriggling animal which was trying to get its paw in under the door. With his mother and Puja awake, there was no time to lose. He had got the spear through the window, and though he could not manoeuvre it so as to strike the panther's head, he brought the sharp end down with considerable force on the animal's rump.

With a roar of pain and rage the man-eater leapt down from the steps and disappeared into the darkness. It did not pause to see what had struck it. Certain that no human could have come upon it in that fashion, it ran fearfully to its lair, howling until the pain subsided.

### VIII

A panther is an enigma. There are occasions when it proves himself to be the most cunning animal under the sun, and yet the very next day it will walk into an obvious trap that no self-respecting jackal would ever go near. One day a panther will prove itself to be a complete coward and run like a hare from a couple of dogs, and the very next it will dash in amongst half a dozen men sitting round a camp fire and inflict terrible injuries on them.

It is not often that a panther is taken by surprise, as its power of sight and hearing are very acute. It is a master at the art of camouflage, and its spotted coat is admirably suited for the purpose. It does not need heavy jungle to hide in. A couple of bushes and the light and shade from surrounding trees are enough to make it almost invisible.

Because the Manjari panther had been fooled by Bisnu, it did not mean that it was a stupid panther. It simply meant that it had been a little careless. And Bisnu and Puja, growing in confidence since their midnight encounter with the animal, became a little careless themselves.

Puja was hoeing the last field above the house and Bisnu, at the other end of the same field, was chopping up several branches of green oak, prior to leaving the wood to dry in the loft. It was late afternoon and the descending sun glinted in patches on the small river. It was a time of day when only the most desperate and daring of man-eaters would be likely to show itself.

Pausing for a moment to wipe the sweat from his brow, Bisnu glanced up at the hillside, and his eye caught sight of a rock on the brown of the hill which seemed unfamiliar to him. Just as he was about to look elsewhere, the round rock began to grow and then alter its shape, and Bisnu watching in fascination was at last able to make out the head and forequarters of the panther. It looked enormous from the angle at which he saw it, and for a moment he thought it was a tiger. But Bisnu knew instinctively that it was the man-eater.

Slowly, the wary beast pulled itself to its feet and began to walk round the side of the great rock. For a second it disappeared and Bisnu wondered if it had gone away. Then it reappeared and the boy was all excitement again. Very slowly and silently the panther walked across the face of the rock until it was in direct line with the corner of the field where Puja was working.

With a thrill of horror Bisnu realized that the panther was stalking his sister. He shook himself free from the spell which had woven itself round him and shouting hoarsely ran forward.

'Run, Puja, run!' he called. 'It's on the hill above you!'

Puja turned to see what Bisnu was shouting about. She saw him gesticulate to the hill behind her, looked up just in time to see the panther crouching for his spring.

With great presence of mind, she leapt down the banking of the field and tumbled into an irrigation ditch.

The springing panther missed its prey, lost its foothold on the slippery shale banking and somersaulted into the ditch a few feet away from Puja. Before the animal could recover from its surprise, Bisnu was dashing down the slope, swinging his axe and shouting, '*Maro, maro!* (Kill, kill!)'

Two men came running across the field. They, too, were armed with axes. Together with Bisnu they made a half-circle around the snarling animal, which turned at bay and plunged at them in order to get away. Puja wriggled along the ditch on her stomach. The men aimed their axes at the panther's head, and Bisnu had the satisfaction of getting in a well-aimed blow between the eyes. The animal then charged straight at one of the men, knocked him over and tried to get at his throat. Just then Sanjay's father arrived with his long spear. He plunged the end of the spear into the panther's neck.

The panther left its victim and ran into the bushes, dragging the spear through the grass and leaving a trail of blood on the ground. The men followed cautiously—all except the man who had been wounded and who lay on the ground, while Puja and the other womenfolk rushed up to help him.

The panther had made for the bed of the stream and Bisnu, Sanjay's father and their companion were able to follow it quite easily. The water was red where the panther had crossed the stream, and the rocks were stained with blood. After they had gone downstream for about a furlong, they found the panther lying still on its side at the edge of the water. It was mortally wounded, but it continued to wave its tail like an angry cat. Then, even the tail lay still.

'It is dead,' said Bisnu. 'It will not trouble us again in this body.'

'Let us be certain,' said Sanjay's father, and he bent down and pulled the panther's tail.

There was no response.

'It is dead,' said Kalam Singh. 'No panther would suffer such an insult were it alive!'

They cut down a long piece of thick bamboo and tied the panther to it by its feet. Then, with their enemy hanging upside down from the bamboo pole, they started back for the village.

'There will be a feast at my house tonight,' said Kalam Singh. 'Everyone in the village must come. And tomorrow we will visit all the villages in the valley and show them the dead panther, so that they may move about again without fear.'

'We can sell the skin in Kemptee,' said their companion. 'It will fetch a good price.'

'But the claws we will give to Bisnu,' said Kalam Singh, putting his arm around the boy's shoulders. 'He has done a man's work today. He deserves the claws.'

A panther's or tiger's claws are considered to be lucky charms.

'I will take only three claws,' said Bisnu. 'One each for my mother and sister, and one for myself. You may give the others to Sanjay and Chittru and the smaller children.'

As the sun set, a big fire was lit in the middle of the village of Manjari and the people gathered round it, singing and laughing. Kalam Singh killed his fattest goat and there was meat for everyone.

IX

Bisnu was on his way home. He had just handed in his first paper, arithmetic, which he had found quite easy. Tomorrow it would be algebra, and when he got home he would have to practice square roots and cube roots and fractional coefficients.

Mr Nautiyal and the entire class had been happy that he had been able to sit for the exams. He was also a hero to them for his part in killing the panther. The story had spread through the villages with the rapidity of a forest fire, a fire which was now raging in Kemptee town.

When he walked past the hospital, he was whistling cheerfully. Dr Taylor waved to him from the veranda steps.

'How is Sanjay now?' she asked.

'He is well,' said Bisnu.

'And your mother and sister?'

'They are well,' said Bisnu.

'Are you going to get yourself a new dog?'

'I am thinking about it,' said Bisnu. 'At present I have a baby goat—I am teaching it to swim!'

He started down the path to the valley. Dark clouds had gathered and there was a rumble of thunder. A storm was imminent.

'Wait for me!' shouted Sarru, running down the path behind Bisnu, his milk pails clanging against each other. He fell into step beside Bisnu.

'Well, I hope we don't have any more man-eaters for some time,' he said. 'I've lost a lot of money by not being able to take milk up to Kemptee.'

'We should be safe as long as a shikari doesn't wound another panther. There was an old bullet wound in the man-eater's thigh. That's why it couldn't hunt in the forest. The deer were too fast for it.'

'Is there a new postman yet?'

'He starts tomorrow. A cousin of Mela Ram's.'

When they reached the parting of their ways it had begun to rain a little.

'I must hurry,' said Sarru. 'It's going to get heavier any minute.' 'I feel like getting wet,' said Bisnu. This time it's the monsoon, I'm sure.'

Bisnu entered the forest on his own, and at the same time the rain came down in heavy opaque sheets. The trees shook in the wind, the langoors chattered with excitement.

It was still pouring when Bisnu emerged from the forest, drenched to the skin. But the rain stopped suddenly, just as the village of Manjari came in view. The sun appeared through a rift in the clouds. The leaves and the grass gave out a sweet, fresh smell.

Bisnu could see his mother and sister in the field transplanting the rice seedlings. The menfolk were driving the yoked oxen through the thin mud of the fields, while the children hung on to the oxen's tails, standing on the plain wooden harrows and with weird cries and shouts sending the animals almost at a gallop along the narrow terraces.

Bisnu felt the urge to be with them, working in the fields. He ran clown the path, his feet falling softly on the wet earth. Puja saw him coming and waved to him. She met him at the edge of the field.

'How did you find your paper today?' she asked.

'Oh, it was easy.' Bisnu slipped his hand into hers and together they walked across the field. Puja felt something smooth and hard against her fingers, and before she could see what Bisnu was doing, he had slipped a pair of bangles over her wrist.

'I remembered,' he said, with a sense of achievement. Puja looked at the bangles and burst out: 'But they are blue, Bhai, and I wanted red and gold bangles!' And then, when she saw him looking crestfallen, she hurried on: 'But they are very pretty, and you did remember... Actually, they're just as nice as red and gold bangles! Come into the house when you are ready. I have made something special for you.'

'I am coming,' said Bisnu, turning towards the house. 'You don't know how hungry a man gets, walking five miles to reach home!'

# FAIRY GLEN PALACE

The old bridle path from Rajpur to Mussoorie passed through Fosterganj at a height of about 5,000 feet. In the old days, before the motor road was built, this was the only road to the hill station. You could ride up on a pony, or walk, or be carried in a basket (if you were a child) or in a doolie (if you were a lady or an invalid). The doolie was a cross between a hammock, a stretcher and a sedan chair, if you can imagine such a contraption. It was borne aloft by two perspiring partners. Sometimes they sat down to rest, and dropped you unceremoniously. I have a picture of my grandmother being borne uphill in a doolie, and she looks petrified. There was an incident in which a doolie, its occupant and two bearers, all went over a cliff just before Fosterganj, and perished in the fall. Sometimes you can see the ghost of this poor lady being borne uphill by two phantom bearers.

Fosterganj has its ghosts, of course. And they are something of a distraction.

Writing is my vocation, and I have always tried to follow the apostolic maxim: 'Study to be quiet and to mind your own business.' But in small-town India one is constantly drawn into other people's business, just as they are drawn towards yours. In Fosterganj it was quiet enough, there were few people; there was no excuse for shirking work. But tales of haunted houses and fairy-infested forests have always intrigued me, and when I heard that the ruined palace halfway down to Rajpur was a place to be avoided after dark, it was natural for me to start taking my evening walks in its direction.

Fairy Glen was its name. It had been built on the lines of a Swiss or French chalet, with numerous turrets decorating its many wings—a huge, rambling building, two-storeyed, with numerous balconies and cornices and windows; a hodge-podge of architectural styles, a wedding-cake of a palace, built to satisfy the whims and fancies of its late owner, the Raja of Ranipur, a small state near the Nepal border. Maintaining this ornate edifice must have been something of a nightmare; and the present heirs had quite given up on it, for bits of the roof were missing, some windows were without panes, doors had developed cracks, and what had once been a garden was now a small jungle. Apparently there was no one living there anymore; no sign of a caretaker. I had walked past the wrought-iron gate several times without seeing any signs of life, apart from a large grey cat sunning itself outside a broken window.

Then one evening, walking up from Rajpur, I was caught in a storm.

A wind had sprung up, bringing with it dark, overburdened clouds. Heavy drops of rain were followed by hailstones bouncing off the stony path. Gusts of wind rushed through the oaks, and leaves and small branches were soon swirling through the air. I was still a couple of miles from the Fosterganj bazaar, and I did not fancy sheltering under a tree, as flashes of lightning were beginning to light up the darkening sky. Then I found myself outside the gate of the abandoned palace.

Outside the gate stood an old sentry box. No one had stood sentry in it for years. It was a good place in which to take shelter. But I hesitated because a large bird was perched on the gate, seemingly oblivious to the rain that was still falling.

It looked like a crow or a raven, but it was much bigger than either—in fact, twice the size of a crow, but having all the features of one—and when a flash of lightning lit up the gate, it gave a squawk, opened its enormous wings and took off, flying in the direction of the oak forest. I hadn't seen such a bird before; there was something dark and malevolent and almost supernatural about it. But it had gone, and I darted into the sentry box without further delay.

I had been standing there some ten minutes, wondering when the rain was going to stop, when I heard someone running down the road. As he approached, I could see that he was just a boy, probably eleven or twelve; but in the dark I could not make out his features. He came up to the gate, lifted the latch, and was about to go in when he saw me in the sentry box.

'Kaun? Who are you?' he asked, first in Hindi then in English. He did not appear to be in any way anxious or alarmed.

'Just sheltering from the rain,' I said. 'I live in the bazaar.'

He took a small torch from his pocket and shone it in my face.

'Yes, I have seen you there.

'A tourist.'

'A writer. I stay in places, I don't just pass through.'

'Do you want to come in?'

I hesitated. It was still raining and the roof of the sentry box was leaking badly.

'Do you live here?' I asked.

'Yes, I am the raja's nephew. I live here with my mother. Come in.' He took me by the hand and led me through the gate. His hand was quite rough and heavy for an eleven or twelve-year-old. Instead of walking with me to the front steps and entrance of the old palace, he led me around to the rear of the building, where a faint light glowed in a mullioned window, and in its light I saw that he had a very fresh and pleasant face—a face as yet untouched by the trials of life.

Instead of knocking on the door, he tapped on the window. 'Only strangers knock on the door,' he said. 'When I tap on the window, my mother knows it's me.'

'That's clever of you,' I said.

He tapped again, and the door was opened by an unusually tall woman wearing a kind of loose, flowing gown that looked strange in that place, and on her. The light was behind her, and I couldn't see her face until we had entered the room. When she turned to me, I saw that she had a long reddish scar running down one side of her face. Even so, there was a certain, hard beauty in her appearance.

'Make some tea—Mother,' said the boy rather brusquely. 'And something to eat. I'm hungry. Sir, will you have something?' He looked enquiringly at me. The light from a kerosene lamp fell full on his face. He was wide-eyed, full-lipped, smiling; only his voice seemed rather mature for one so young. And he spoke like someone much older, and with an almost unsettling sophistication.

'Sit down, sir.' He led me to a chair, made me comfortable. 'You are not too wet, I hope?'

'No, I took shelter before the rain came down too heavily. But you are wet, you'd better change.'

'It doesn't bother me.' And after a pause, 'Sorry there is no electricity. Bills haven't been paid for years.'

'Is this your place?'

'No, we are only caretakers. Poor relations, you might say. The palace has been in dispute for many years. The raja and his brothers keep fighting over it, and meanwhile, it is slowly falling down. The lawyers are happy. Perhaps I should study and become a lawyer some day.'

'Do you go to school?'

'Sometimes.'

'How old are you?'

'Quite old, I'm not sure. Mother, how old am I?' he asked, as the tall woman returned with cups of tea and a plate full of biscuits.

She hesitated, gave him a puzzled look. 'Don't you know? It's on your certificate.'

'I've lost the certificate.'

'No, I've kept it safely.' She looked at him intently, placed a hand on his shoulder, then turned to me and said, 'He is twelve,' with a certain finality.

We finished our tea. It was still raining.

'It will rain all night,' said the boy. 'You had better stay here.'

'It will inconvenience you.'

'No, it won't. There are many rooms. If you do not mind the darkness. Come, I will show you everything. And meanwhile my mother will make some dinner. Very simple food, I hope you won't mind.'

The boy took me around the old palace, if you could still call it that. He led the way with a candle-holder from which a large candle threw our exaggerated shadows on the walls.

'What's your name?' I asked, as he led me into what must have been a reception room, still crowded with ornate furniture and bric-a-brac.

'Bhim,' he said. 'But everyone calls me Lucky.'

'And are you lucky?'

He shrugged. 'Don't know…' Then he smiled up at me. 'Maybe you'll bring me luck.'

We walked further into the room. Large oil paintings hung from the walls, gathering mould. Some were portraits of royalty, kings and queens of another era, wearing decorative headgear, strange uniforms, the women wrapped in jewellery—more jewels than garments, it seemed—and sometimes accompanied by children who were also weighed down by excessive clothing. A young man sat on a throne, his lips curled in a sardonic smile.

'My grandfather,' said Bhim.

He led me into a large bedroom taken up by a four-poster bed which had probably seen several royal couples copulating upon it. It looked cold and uninviting, but Bhim produced a voluminous razai from a cupboard and assured me that it would be warm and quite luxurious, as it had been his grandfather's.

'And when did your grandfather die?' I asked.

'Oh, fifty-sixty years ago, it must have been.'

'In this bed, I suppose.'

'No, he was shot accidentally while out hunting. They said it was an accident. But he had enemies.'

'Kings have enemies... And this was the royal bed?'

He gave me a sly smile; not so innocent after all. 'Many women slept in it. He had many queens.'

'And concubines.'

'What are concubines?'

'Unofficial queens.'

'Yes, those too.'

A worldly-wise boy of twelve.

# THE TWO CAPTIVE POLICEMEN, INSPECTOR HUKAM SINGH AND SUB-INSPECTOR GULER SINGH

Inspector Hukam Singh and Sub-inspector Guler Singh, were being pushed unceremoniously along the dusty, deserted, sun-drenched road. The people of the village had made themselves scarce. They would reappear only when the dacoits went away.

The leader of the dacoit gang was Mangal Singh Bundela, great-grandson of a Pindari adventurer who had been a thorn in the side of the British. Mangal was doing his best to be a thorn in the flesh of his own government. The local police force had been strengthened recently but it was still inadequate for dealing with the dacoits who knew the ravines better than any surveyor. The dacoit Mangal had made a fortune out of ransom. His chief victims were the sons of wealthy industrialists, moneylenders and landowners. But today he had captured two police officials; of no value as far as ransom went, but prestigious prisoners who could be put to other uses...

Mangal Singh wanted to show off in front of the police. He would kill at least one of them—his reputation demanded it but he would let the other go, in order that his legendary power and ruthlessness be given maximum publicity. A legend is always a help!

His red-and-green turban was tied rakishly to one side. His dhoti extended right down to his ankles. His slippers were embroidered with gold and silver thread. His weapon was not ancient matchlock but a well-greased .303 rifle. Two of his men had similar rifles. Some had revolvers. Only the smaller fry carried swords or country-made pistols. Mangal Singh's gang, though traditional in many ways, was up-to-date in the matter of weapons. Right now they had the policemen's guns too.

'Come along, Inspector Sahib,' said Mangal Singh, in tones of police barbarity, tugging at the rope that encircled the stout inspector's midriff. 'Had you captured me today, you would have been a hero. You would have taken all the credit even though you could not keep up with your men in the ravines. Too bad you chose to remain sitting in your jeep with the sub-inspector. The jeep will be useful to us. You will not. But I would like you to be a hero all the same and there is none better than a dead hero!' Mangal Singh's followers doubled up with laughter. They loved their leader's cruel sense of humour.

'As for you, Guler Singh,' he continued, giving his attention to the Sub-inspector, 'you are a man from my own village. You should have joined me long ago. But you were never to be trusted. You thought there would be better pickings in the police, didn't you?'

Guler Singh said nothing, simply hung his head and wondered what his fate would be. He felt certain that Mangal Singh would devise some diabolical and fiendish method of dealing with his captives. Guler Singh's only hope was Constable Ghanshyam, who hadn't been caught by the dacoits because, at the time of the ambush, he had been in the bushes relieving himself.

'To the mango tope,' said Mangal Singh, prodding the

policemen forward.

'Listen to me, Mangal,' said the perspiring inspector, who was ready to try anything to get out of his predicament. 'Let me go and I give you my word there'll he no trouble for you in this area as long as I am posted here. What could be more convenient than that?'

'Nothing,' said Mangal Singh. 'But your word isn't good. My word is different. I have told my men that I will hang you at the mango tope and I mean to keep my word. But I believe in fair play—I like a little sport! You may yet go free if your friend here, Sub-Inspector Guler Singh, has his wits about him.'

The inspector and his subordinate exchanged doubtful puzzled looks. They were not to remain puzzled for long. On reaching the mango tope, the dacoits produced a good strong hempen rope, one end looped into a slip knot. Many a garland of marigolds had the inspector received during his mediocre career. Now, for the first time, he was being garlanded with a hangman's noose. He had seen hangings, he had rather enjoyed them, but he had no stomach for his own. The inspector begged for mercy. Who wouldn't have in his position?

'Be quiet,' commanded Mangal Singh. 'I do not want to know about your wife and your children and the manner in which they will starve. You shot my son last year.'

'Not I!' cried the inspector. 'It was some other.'

'You led the party. But now, just to show you that I'm a sporting fellow, I am going to have you strung up from this tree and then I am going to give Guler Singh six shots with a rifle, and if he can sever the rope that suspends you before you are dead, well then, you can remain alive and I will let you go! For your sake I hope the sub-inspector's aim is good. He will have to shoot fast. My man Phambiri, who has made this noose, was once the executioner in a city jail. He guarantees that you won't last more than fifteen seconds at the end of his rope.'

Guler Singh was taken to a spot about forty yards away. A rifle was thrust into his hands. Two dacoits clambered into the branches of the mango tree. The inspector, his hands tied behind, could only gaze at them in horror. His mouth opened and shut as though he already had need of more air. And then, suddenly, the rope went taut, up went the inspector, his throat caught in a vice, while the branch of the tree shook and mango blossoms fluttered to the ground. The inspector dangled from the rope, his feet about three feet above the ground.

'You can shoot,' said Mangal Singh, nodding to the sub inspector.

And Guler Singh, his hands trembling a little, raised the rifle to his shoulder and fired three shots in rapid succession. But the rope was swinging violently and the inspector's body was jerking about like a fish on a hook. The bullets went wide.

Guler Singh found the magazine empty. He reloaded, wiped the stinging sweat from his *eyes,* raised the rifle again, took more careful aim. His hands were steadier now. He rested the sights on the upper portion of the rope, where there was less motion. Normally he was a good shot but he had never been asked to demonstrate his skill in circumstances such as these.

The inspector still gyrated at the end of his rope. There was life in him yet. His face was purple. The world, in those choking moments, was a medley of upside-down roofs and a red sun spinning slowly towards him.

Guler Singh's rifle cracked again. An inch or two wide this time. But the fifth shot found its mark, sending small tuffs of rope winging into the air.

The shot did not sever the rope; it was only a nick. Guler Singh had one shot left. He was quite calm. The rifle Sight followed the rope's swing, less agitated now that the inspector's convulsions were lessening. Guler Singh felt sure he could sever the rope this time.

And then, as his finger touched the trigger, an odd, disturbing thought slipped into his mind, stayed there, throbbing. 'Whose life are you trying to save? Hukam Singh has stood in the way of your promotion more than once. He had you chargesheeted for accepting fifty rupees from an unlicensed rickshaw puller. He makes you do all the dirty work, blames you when things go wrong, takes the credit when there is credit to be taken. But for him, you'd be an inspector!'

The rope swayed slightly to the right. The rifle moved just a fraction to the left. The last shot rang out, clipping a sliver of bark from the mango tree.

The inspector was dead when they cut him down.

'Bad luck,' said Mangal Singh Bundela. 'You nearly saved him. But the next time I catch up with you, Guler Singh, it will be your turn to hang from the mango tree. So keep well away! You know that I am a man of my word. I keep it now by giving you your freedom.'

A few minutes later the party of dacoits had melted away into the late afternoon shadows of the scrub forest. There was the sound of a jeep starting up. Then silence—a silence so profound that it seemed to be shouting in Guler Singh's ears.

As the village people began to trickle out of their houses, Constable Ghanshyam appeared as if from nowhere, swearing that he had lost his way in the jungle. Several people had seen the incident from their windows. They were unanimous in praising the sub-inspector for his brave attempt to save his superior's life. He had done his best.

'It is true,' thought Guler Singh. 'I did my best.'

That moment of hesitation before the last shot, the question that had suddenly reared up in the darkness of his mind, was already gone from his memory. We remember only what we want to remember.

'I did my best,' he told everyone.

And so he had.

# THE ROOM OF MANY COLOURS

Last week I wrote a story, and all the time I was writing it, I thought it was a good story; but when it was finished and I had read it through, I found that there was something missing, that it didn't ring true. So I tore it up. I wrote a poem, about an old man sleeping in the sun, and this was true, but it was finished quickly, and once again I was left with the problem of what to write next. And I remembered my father, who taught me to write; and I thought, why not write about my father, and about the trees we planted, and about the people I knew while growing up and about what happened on the way to growing up.

And so, like Alice, I must begin at the beginning, and in the beginning there was this red insect, just like a velvet button, which I found on the front lawn of the bungalow. The grass was still wet with overnight rain.

I placed the insect on the palm of my hand and took it into the house to show my father.

'Look, Dad,' I said, 'I haven't seen an insect like this before. Where has it come from?'

'Where did you find it?' he asked. 'On the grass.'

'It must have come down from the sky,' he said. 'It must have come down with the rain.'

Later he told me how the insect really happened but I preferred his first explanation. It was more fun to have it dropping from the sky.

I was seven at the time, and my father was thirty-seven, but, right from the beginning, he made me feel that I was old enough to talk to him about everything—insects, people, trees, steam engines, King George, comics, crocodiles, the Mahatma, the Viceroy, America, Mozambique and Timbuctoo. We took long walks together, explored old ruins, chased butterflies and waved to passing trains.

My mother had gone away when I was four, and I had very dim memories of her. Most other children had their mothers with them, and I found it a bit strange that mine couldn't stay. Whenever I asked my father why she'd gone, he'd say, 'You'll understand when you grow up.' And if I asked him *where* she'd gone, he'd look troubled and say, 'I really don't know.' This was the only question of mine to which he didn't have an answer.

But I was quite happy living alone with my father; I had never known any other kind of life.

We were sitting on an old wall, looking out to sea at a couple of Arab dhows and a tram steamer, when my father said, 'Would you like to go to sea one day?'

'Where does the sea go?' I asked.

'It goes everywhere.'

'Does it go to the end of the world?'

'It goes right round the world. It's a round world.'

'It can't be.'

'It is. But it's so big, you can't see the roundness. When a fly sits on a watermelon, it can't see right round the melon, can it? The melon must seem quite flat to the fly. Well, in comparison to the world, we're much, much smaller than the tiniest of insects.'

'Have you been around the world?' I asked.

'No, only as far as England. That's where your grandfather was born.'

'And my grandmother?'

'She came to India from Norway when she was quite small. Norway is a cold land, with mountains and snow, and the sea cutting deep into the land. I was there as a boy. It's very beautiful, and the people are good and work hard.'

'I'd like to go there.'

'You will, one day. When you are older, I'll take you to Norway.'

'Is it better than England?'

'It's quite different.'

'Is it better than India?'

'It's quite different.'

'Is India like England?'

'No, it's different.'

'Well, what does "different" mean?'

'It means things are not the same. It means people are different. It means the weather is different. It means tree and birds and insects are different.'

'Are English crocodiles different from Indian crocodiles?'

'They don't have crocodiles in England.'

'Oh, then it must be different.'

'It would be a dull world if it was the same everywhere,' said my father.

He never lost patience with my endless questioning. If he wanted a rest, he would take out his pipe and spend a long time lighting it. If this took very long I'd find something else to do. But sometimes I'd wait patiently until the pipe was drawing, and then return to the attack.

'Will we always be in India?' I asked.

'No, we'll have to go away one day. You see, it's hard to explain, but it isn't really our country.'

'Ayah says it belongs to the king of England, and the jewels in his crown were taken from India, and that when the Indians get their jewels back the king will lose India! But first they have to get the crown from the king, but this is very difficult, she says, because the crown is always on his head. He even sleeps wearing his crown!'

Ayah was my nanny. She loved me deeply, and was always filling my head with strange and wonderful stories. My father did not comment on Ayah's views. All he said was,

'We'll have to go away some day.'

'How long have we been here?' I asked.

'Two hundred years.'

'No, I mean us.'

'Well, you were born in India, so that's seven years for you.'

'Then can't I stay here?'

'Do you want to?'

'I want to go across the sea. But can we take Ayah with us?'

'I don't know, son. Let's walk along the beach.'

We lived in an old palace beside a lake. The palace looked like a ruin from the outside, but the rooms were cool and comfortable. We lived in one wing, and my father organized a small school in another wing. His pupils were the children of the raja and the raja's relatives. My father had started life in India as a tea planter, but he had been trained as a teacher and the idea of starting a school in a small state facing the Arabian Sea had appealed to him. The pay wasn't much, but we had a palace to live in, the latest 1938 model Hillman to drive about in, and a number of servants. In those days, of course, everyone had servants (although the servants did not have any!). Ayah was our own; but the cook, the bearer, the gardener, and the bhisti were all provided by the state. Sometimes I sat in the schoolroom with the other children (who were all much bigger than me), sometimes I remained in the house with Ayah, sometimes I followed the gardener, Dukhi, about the spacious garden.

Dukhi means 'sad', and though I never could discover if the gardener had anything to feel sad about, the name certainly suited him. He had grown to resemble the drooping weeds that he was always digging up with a tiny spade. I seldom saw him standing up. He always sat on the ground with his knees well up to his chin, and attacked the weeds from this position. He could spend all day on his haunches, moving about the garden simply by shuffling his feet along the grass.

I tried to imitate his posture, sitting down on my heels and putting my knees into my armpits, but could never hold the position for more than five minutes.

Time had no meaning in a large garden, and Dukhi never hurried. Life, for him, was not a matter of one year succeeding another, but of five seasons—winter, spring, hot weather, monsoon and autumn—arriving and departing. His seedbeds had always to be in readiness for the coming season, and he did not look any further than the next monsoon. It was impossible to tell his age. He may have been thirty-six or eighty-six. He was either very young for his years or very old for them.

Dukhi loved bright colours, especially reds and yellows. He liked strongly scented flowers, like jasmine and honeysuckle. He couldn't understand my father's preference for the more delicately perfumed petunias and sweetpeas. But I shared Dukhi's fondness for the common bright orange marigold, which is offered in temples and is used to make garlands and nosegays. When the garden was bare of all colour, the marigold would still be there, gay and flashy, challenging the sun.

Dukhi was very fond of making nosegays, and I liked to

watch him at work. A sunflower formed the centrepiece. It was surrounded by roses, marigolds and oleander, fringed with green leaves, and bound together with silver thread. The perfume was overpowering. The nosegays were presented to me or my father on special occasions, that is, on a birthday or to guests of my father's who were considered important.

One day I found Dukhi making a nosegay, and said, 'No one is coming today, Dukhi. It isn't even a birthday.'

'It is a birthday, Chota Sahib,' he said. 'Little Sahib' was the title he had given me. It wasn't much of a title compared to Raja Sahib, Diwan Sahib or Burra Sahib, but it was nice to have a title at the age of seven.

'Oh,' I said, 'And is there a party, too?'

'No party.'

'What's the use of a birthday without a party? What's the use of a birthday without presents?'

'This person doesn't like presents—just flowers.'

'Who is it?' I asked, full of curiosity.

'If you want to find out, you can take these flowers to her. She lives right at the top of that far side of the palace. There are twenty-two steps to climb. Remember that, Chota Sahib, you take twenty-three steps and you will go over the edge and into the lake!'

I started climbing the stairs.

It was a spiral staircase of wrought iron, and it went round and round and up and up, and it made me quite dizzy and tired.

At the top I found myself on a small balcony, which looked out over the lake and another palace, at the crowded *city* and the distant harbour. I heard a voice, a rather high, musical voice, saying (in English), 'Are you a ghost?' I turned to see who had spoken but found the balcony empty. The voice had come from a dark room.

I turned to the stairway, ready to flee, but the voice said, 'Oh, don't go, there's nothing to be frightened of!'

And so I stood still, peering cautiously into the darkness of the room.

'First, tell me—are you a ghost?'

'I'm a boy,' I said.

'And I'm a girl. We can he friends. I can't come out there, so you had better come in. Come along, I'm not a ghost either—not yet, anyway!'

As there was nothing very frightening about the voice, I stepped into the room. It was dark inside, and, coming in from the glare, it took me some time to make out the tiny, elderly lady seated on a cushioned gilt chair. She wore a red sari, lots of coloured bangles on her wrists, and golden earrings. Her hair was streaked with white, but her skin was still quite smooth and unlined, and she had large and very beautiful eyes.

'You must be Master Bond!' she said. 'Do you know who I am?'

'You're a lady with a birthday,' I said, 'but that's all I know. Dukhi didn't tell me any more.'

'If you promise to keep it secret, I'll tell you who I am. You see, everyone thinks I'm mad. Do you think so too?'

'I don't know.'

'Well, you must tell me if you think so,' she said with a chuckle. Her laugh was the sort of sound made by the gecko, a little wall lizard, coming from deep down in the throat. 'I have a feeling you are a truthful boy. Do you find it very difficult to tell the truth?'

'Sometimes.'

'Sometimes. Of course, there are times when I tell lies—lots of little lies—because they're such fun! But would you call me a liar? I wouldn't, if I were you, but *would* you?'

'Are you a liar?'

'I'm asking you! If I were to tell you that I was a queen—that *I am* a queen—would you believe me?'

I thought deeply about this, and then said, 'I'll try to believe you.'

'Oh, but you *must* believe me. I'm a real queen, I'm a rani! Look, I've got diamonds to prove it!' And she held out her hands, and there was a ring on each finger, the stones glowing and glittering in the dim light. 'Diamonds, rubies, pearls and emeralds! Only a queen can have these!' She was most anxious that I should believe her.

'You must be a queen,' I said.

'Right!' she snapped. 'In that case, would you mind calling me, "Your Highness"?'

'Your Highness,' I said.

She smiled. It was a slow, beautiful smile. Her whole face lit up. 'I could love you,' she said. 'But better still, I'll give you something to eat. Do you like chocolates?'

'Yes, Your Highness.'

'Well,' she said, taking a box from the table beside her, 'these have come all the way from England. Take two. Only two, mind, otherwise the box will finish before Thursday, and I don't want that to happen because I won't get any more till Saturday. That's when Captain MacWhirr's ship gets in, the *SS Lucy*, loaded with boxes and boxes of chocolates!'

'All for you?' I asked in considerable awe.

'Yes, of course. They have to last at least three months. I get them from England. I get only the best chocolates. I like them with pink, crunchy fillings, don't you?'

'Oh, yes!' I exclaimed, full of envy.

'Never mind,' she said. 'I may give you one, now and then—if you're very nice to me! Here you are, help yourself...' She pushed the chocolate box towards me.

I took a silver-wrapped chocolate, and then just as I was thinking of taking a second, she quickly took the box away.

'No more!' she said. 'They have to last till Saturday.'

'But I took only one,' I said with some indignation.

'Did you?' She gave me a sharp look, decided I was telling the truth, and said graciously, 'Well, in that case you can have another.'

Watching the Rani carefully, in case she snatched the box away again, I selected a second chocolate, this one with a green wrapper. I don't remember what kind of day it was outside, but I remember the bright green of the chocolate wrapper.

I thought it would be rude to eat the chocolates in front of a queen, so I put them in my pocket and said, 'I'd better go now. Ayah will be looking for me.'

'And when will you be coming to see me again?'

'I don't know,' I said.

'Your Highness.'

'Your Highness.'

'There's something I want you to do for me,' she said, placing one finger on my shoulder and giving me a conspiratorial look. 'Will you do it?'

'What is it, Your Highness?'

'What is it? Why do you ask? A real prince never asks where or why or whatever, he simply does what the princess asks of him. When I was a princess—before I became a queen, that is—I asked a prince to swim across the lake and fetch me a lily growing on the other bank.'

'And did he get it for you?'

'He drowned halfway across. Let that he a lesson to you. Never agree to do something without knowing what it is.'

'But I thought you said...'

'Never mind what I *said*. It's what I say that matters!'

'Oh, all right,' I said, fidgeting to be gone. 'What is it you want me to do?'

'Nothing.' Her tiny rosebud lips pouted and she stared sullenly at a picture on the wall. Now that my eyes had grown used to the dim light in the room, I noticed that the walls were hung with portraits of stout rajas and ranis turbaned and bedecked in fine clothes. There were also portraits of Queen Victoria and King George V of England. And, in the centre of all this distinguished company, a large picture of Mickey Mouse.

'I'll do it if it isn't too dangerous,' I said.

'Then listen.' She took my hand and drew me towards her—what a tiny hand she had!—and whispered, 'I want a red rose. From the palace garden. But be careful! Don't let Dukhi the gardener catch you. He'll know it's for me. He knows I love roses. And he hates me! I'll tell you why, one day. But if he catches you, he'll do something terrible.'

'To me?'

'No, to himself. That's much worse, isn't it? He'll tie himself into knots, or lie naked on a bed of thorns, or go on a long fast with nothing to eat but fruit, sweets and chicken! So you will be careful, won't you?'

'Oh, but he doesn't hate you,' I cried in protest, remembering the flowers he'd sent for her, and looking around I found that I'd been sitting on them. 'Look, he sent these flowers for your birthday!'

'Well, if he sent them for my birthday, you can take them back,' she snapped. 'But if he sent them for me...' and she suddenly softened and looked coy, 'then I might keep them. Thank you, my dear, it was a very sweet thought.' And she learnt forward as though to kiss me.

'It's late, I must go!' I said in alarm, and turning on my

heels, ran out of the room and down the spiral staircase.

Father hadn't started lunch, or rather tiffin, as we called it then. He usually waited for me if I was late. I don't suppose he enjoyed eating alone.

For tiffin we usually had rice, a mutton curry (koftas or meat balls, with plenty of gravy, was my favourite curry), fried dal and a hot lime or mango pickle. For supper we had English food—a soup, roast pork and fried potatoes, a rich gravy made by my father, and a custard or caramel pudding. My father enjoyed cooking, but it was only in the morning that he found time for it. Breakfast was his own creation. He cooked eggs in a variety of interesting ways, and favoured some Italian recipes which he had collected during a trip to Europe, long before I was born.

In deference to the feelings of our Hindu friends, we did not eat beef; but, apart from mutton and chicken, there was a plentiful supply of other meats—partridge, venison, lobster, and even porcupine!

'And where have you been?' asked my father, helping himself to the rice as soon as he saw me come in.

'To the top of the old palace,' I said.

'Did you meet anyone there?'

'Yes, I met a tiny lady who told me she was a rani. She gave me chocolates.'

'As a rule, she doesn't like visitors.'

'Oh, she didn't mind me. But is she really a queen?'

'Well, she's the daughter of a maharaja. That makes her a princess. She never married. There's a story that she fell in love with a commoner, one of the palace servants, and wanted to marry him, but of course they wouldn't allow that. She became very melancholic, and started living all by herself in the old palace.

They give her everything she needs, but she doesn't go out or have visitors. Everyone says she's mad.'

'How do they know?' I asked.

'Because she's different from other people, I suppose.'

'Is that being mad?'

'No. Not really, I suppose madness is not seeing things as others see them.'

'Is that very bad?'

'No,' said Father, who for once was finding it very difficult to explain something to me. 'But people who are like that—people whose minds are so different that they don't think, step by step, as we do, whose thoughts jump all over the place—such people are difficult to live with.'

'Step by step,' I repeated. 'Step by step.'

'You aren't eating,' said my father. 'Hurry up, and you can come with me to school today.'

I always looked forward to attending my father's classes. He did not take me to the schoolroom very often, because he wanted school to be a treat, to begin with, and then, later, the routine wouldn't be so unwelcome.

Sitting there with older children, understanding only half of what they were learning, I felt important and part grown-up. And of course I did learn to read and write, although I first learnt to read upside-down, by means of standing in front of the others' desks and peering across at their books. Later, when I went to school, I had some difficulty in learning to read the right way up; and even today I sometimes read upside-down, for the sake of variety. I don't mean that I read standing on my head; simply that I held the book upside-down.

I had at my command a number of rhymes and jingles, the most interesting of these being 'Solomon Grundy'.

*Solomon Grundy,*
*Born on a Monday,*
*Christened on Tuesday,*
*Married on Wednesday,*
*Took ill on Thursday,*
*Worse on Friday,*
*Died on Saturday,*
*Buried on Sunday:*
*This is the end of*
*Solomon Grundy.*

Was that all that life amounted to, in the end? And were we all Solomon Grundys? These were questions that bothered me at the time. Another puzzling rhyme was the one that went:

*Hark, hark,*
*The dogs do hark,*
*The beggars are coming to town;*
*Some in rags,*
*Some in bags,*
*And some in velvet gowns.*

This rhyme puzzled me for a long time. There were beggars aplenty in the bazaar, and sometimes they came to the house, and some of then, did wear rags and bags (and some nothing at all) and the dogs did bark at them, but the beggar in the velvet gown never came our way.

'Who's this beggar in a velvet gown?' I asked my father.

'Not a beggar at all,' he said.

'Then why call him one?'

And I went to Ayah and asked her the same question, 'Who is the beggar in the velvet gown?'

'Jesus Christ,' said Ayah.

Ayah was a fervent Christian and made me say my prayers at night, even when I was very sleepy. She had, I think, Arab and Negro blood in addition to the blood of the Koli fishing community to which her mother had belonged. Her father, a sailor on an Arab dhow, had been a convert to Christianity. Ayah was a large, buxom woman, with heavy hands and feet and a slow, swaying gait that had all the grace and majesty of a royal elephant. Elephants for all their size are nimble creatures; and Ayah, too, was nimble, sensitive, and gentle with her big hands. Her face was always sweet and childlike.

Although a Christian, she clung to many of the beliefs of her parents, and loved to tell me stories about mischievous spirits and evil spirits, humans who changed into animals, and snakes who had been princes in their former lives.

There was the story of the snake who married a princess. At first the princess did not wish to marry the snake, whom she had met in a forest, but the snake insisted, saying, 'I'll kill you if you won't marry me,' and of course that settled the question. The snake led his bride away and took her to a great treasure. 'I was a prince in my former life,' he explained. 'This treasure is yours.' And then the snake very gallantly disappeared.

'Snakes,' declared Ayah, 'were very lucky omens if seen early in the morning.'

'But, what if the snake bites the lucky person?' I asked.

'He will be lucky all the same,' said Ayah with a logic that was all her own.

Snakes! There were a number of them living in the big garden, and my father had advised me to avoid the long grass. But I had seen snakes crossing the road (a lucky omen, according to Ayah) and they were never aggressive.

'A snake won't attack you,' said Father, 'provided you leave it alone. Of course, if you step on one it will probably bite.'

'Are all snakes poisonous?'

'Yes, but only a few are poisonous enough to kill a man. Others use their poison on rats and frogs. A good thing, too, otherwise during the rains the house would be taken over by the frogs.'

One afternoon, while Father was at school, Ayah found a snake in the bathtub. It wasn't early morning and so the snake couldn't have been a lucky one. Ayah was frightened and ran into the garden calling for help. Dukhi came running. Ayah ordered me to stay outside while they went after the snake.

And it was while I was alone in the garden—an unusual circumstance, since Dukhi was nearly always there—that I remembered the Rani's request. On an impulse, I went to the nearest rose bush and plucked the largest rose, pricking my thumb in the process.

And then, without waiting to see what had happened to the snake (it finally escaped), I started up the steps to the top of the old palace.

When I got to the top, I knocked on the door of the Rani's room. Getting no reply, I walked along the balcony until I reached another doorway. There were wooden panels around the door, with elephants, camels and turbaned warriors carved into it. As the door was open, I walked boldly into the room then stood still in astonishment. The room was filled with a strange light. There were windows going right round the room, and each small windowpane was made of a different coloured glass. The sun that came through one window flung red and green and purple colours on the figure of the little Rani who stood there with her face pressed to the glass.

She spoke to me without turning from the window. 'This is my favourite room. I have all the colours here. I can see a different world through each pane of glass. Come, join me!' And she beckoned to me, her small hand fluttering like a delicate butterfly.

I went up to the Rani. She was only a little taller than me, and we were able to share the same windowpane.

'See, it's a red world!' she said.

The garden below, the palace and the lake, were all tinted red. I watched the Rani's world for a little while and then touched her on the arm and said, 'I have brought you a rose!'

She started away from me, and her eyes looked frightened. She would not look at the rose.

'Oh, why did you bring it?' she cried, wringing her hands. 'He'll be arrested now!'

'Who'll be arrested?'

'The prince, of course!'

'But *I* took it,' I said. 'No one saw me. Ayah and Dukhi were inside the house, catching a snake.'

'Did they catch it?' she asked, forgetting about the rose.

'I don't know. I didn't wait to see!'

'They should follow the snake, instead of catching it. It may lead them to a treasure. All snakes have treasures to guard.'

This seemed to confirm what Ayah had been telling me, and I resolved that I would follow the next snake that I met.

'Don't you like the rose, then?' I asked.

'Did you steal it?'

'Yes.'

'Good. Flowers should always be stolen. They're more fragrant then.'

Because of a man called Hitler war had been declared in Europe and Britain was fighting Germany.

In my comic papers, the Germans were usually shown as blundering idiots; so I didn't see how Britain could possibly lose the war, nor why it should concern India, nor why it should be necessary for my father to join up. But I remember his showing me a newspaper headline which said:

BOMBS FALL ON BUCKINGHAM PALACE—KING AND QUEEN SAFE

I expect that had something to do with it.

He went to Delhi for an interview with the RAF and I was left in Ayah's charge.

It was a week I remember well, because it was the first time I had been left on my own. That first night I was afraid—afraid of the dark, afraid of the emptiness of the house, afraid of the howling of the jackals outside. The loud ticking of the clock was the only reassuring sound: clocks really made themselves heard in those days! I tried concentrating on the ticking, shutting out other sounds and the menace of the dark, but it wouldn't work. I thought I heard a faint hissing near the bed, and sat up, bathed in perspiration, certain that a snake was in the room. I shouted for Ayah and she came running, switching on all the lights.

'A snake!' I cried. 'There's a snake in the room!'

'Where, baba?'

'I don't know where, but I *heard* it.'

Ayah looked under the bed, and behind the chairs and tables, but there was no snake to be found. She persuaded me that I must have heard the breeze whispering in the mosquito curtains.

But I didn't want to be left alone.

'I'm coming to you,' I said and followed her into her small room near the kitchen.

Ayah slept on a low string cot. The mattress was thin, the blanket worn and patched up; but Ayah's warm and solid body made up for the discomfort of the bed. I snuggled up to her and was soon asleep.

I had almost forgotten the Rani in the old palace and was

about to pay her a visit when, to my surprise, I found her in the garden. I had risen early that morning, and had gone running barefoot over the dew-drenched grass. No one was about, but I startled a flock of parrots and the birds rose screeching from a banyan tree and wheeled away to some other corner of the palace grounds. I was just in time to see a mongoose scurrying across the grass with an egg in its mouth. The mongoose must have been raiding the poultry farm at the palace.

I was trying to locate the mongoose's hideout, and was on all fours in a jungle of tall cosmos plants when I heard the rustle of clothes, and turned to find the Rani staring at me.

She didn't ask me what I was doing there, but simply said: 'I don't think he could have gone in there.'

'But I saw him go this way,' I said.

'Nonsense! He doesn't live in this part of the garden. He lives in the roots of the banyan tree.'

'But that's where the snake lives,' I said

'You mean the snake who was a prince. Well, that's whom I'm looking for!'

'A snake who was a prince!' I gaped at the Rani.

She made a gesture of impatience with her butterfly hands, and said, 'Tut, you're only a child, you can't *understand*. The prince lives in the roots of the banyan tree, but he comes out early every morning. Have you seen him?'

'No. But I saw a mongoose.'

The Rani became frightened. 'Oh dear, is there a mongoose in the garden? He might kill the prince!'

'How can a mongoose kill a prince?' I asked.

'You don't understand, Master Bond. Princes, when they die, are born again as snakes.'

'*All* princes?'

'No, only those who die before they can marry.'

'Did your prince die before he could marry you?'

'Yes. And he returned to this garden in the form of a beautiful snake.'

'Well,' I said, 'I hope it wasn't the snake the water carrier killed last week.'

'He killed a snake!' The Rani looked horrified. She was quivering all over. 'It might have been the prince!'

'It was a brown snake,' I said.

'Oh, then it wasn't him.' She looked very relieved. 'Brown snakes are only ministers and people like that. It has to be a green snake to be a prince.'

'I haven't seen any green snakes here.'

'There's one living in the roots of the hanyan tree. You won't kill it, will you?'

'Not if it's really a prince.'

'And you won't let others kill it?'

'I'll tell Ayah.'

'Good. You're on my side. But be careful of the gardener. Keep him away from the hanyan tree. He's always killing snakes. I don't trust him at all.'

She came nearer and, leaning forward a little, looked into my eyes.

'Blue eyes—I trust them. But don't trust green eyes. And yellow eyes are evil.'

'I've never seen yellow eyes.'

'That's because you're pure,' she said, and turned away and hurried across the lawn as though she had just remembered a very urgent appointment.

The sun was up, slanting through the branches of the banyan tree, and Ayah's voice could be heard calling me for breakfast.

'Dukhi,' I said, when I found him in the garden later that day, 'Dukhi, don't kill the snake in the banyan tree.'

'A snake in the banyan tree!' he exclaimed, seizing his hose.

'No, no!' I said. 'I haven't seen it. But the Rani says there's one. She says it was a prince in its former life, and that we shouldn't kill it.'

'Oh,' said Dukhi, smiling to himself. 'The Rani says so. All right, you tell her we won't kill it.'

'Is it true that she was in love with a prince but that he died before she could marry him?'

'Something like that,' said Dukhi. 'It was a long time ago—before I came here.'

'My father says it wasn't a prince, but a commoner. Are you a commoner, Dukhi?'

'A commoner? What's that, Chota Sahib?'

'I'm not sure. Someone very poor, I suppose.'

'Then I must be a commoner,' said Dukhi.

'Were you in love with the Rani?' I asked.

Dukhi was so startled that he dropped his hose and lost his balance; the first time I'd seen him lose his poise while squatting on his haunches.

'Don't say such things, Chota Sahib!'

'Why not?'

'You'll get me into trouble.'

'Then it must be true.'

Dukhi threw up his hands in mock despair and started collecting his implements.

'It's true, it's true!' I cried, dancing round him, and then I ran indoors to Ayah and said, 'Ayah, Dukhi was in love with the Rani!'

Ayah gave a shriek of laughter, then looked very serious and put her finger against my lips.

'Don't say such things,' she said. 'Dukhi is of a very low caste. People won't like it if they hear what you say. And besides, the Rani told you her prince died and turned into a snake. Well, Dukhi hasn't become a snake as yet, has he?'

True, Dukhi didn't look as though he could be anything but a gardener; but I wasn't satisfied with his denials or with Ayah's attempts to still my tongue. Hadn't Dukhi sent the Rani a nosegay?

When my father came home, he looked quite pleased with himself.

'What have you brought for me?' was the first question I asked.

He had brought me some new books, a dartboard, and a train set; and in my excitement over examining these gifts, I forgot to ask about the result of his trip.

It was during tiffin that he told me what had happened and what was going to happen.

'We'll be going away soon' he said. 'I've joined the Royal Air Force. I'll have to work in Delhi.'

'Oh! Will you be in the war, Dad? Will you fly a plane?'

'No, I'm too old to be flying planes. I'll be forty years old in July. The RAF will be giving me what they call intelligence work decoding secret messages and things like that and I don't suppose I'll be able to tell you much about it.'

This didn't sound as exciting as flying planes, but it sounded important and rather mysterious.

'Well, I hope it's interesting,' I said. 'Is Delhi a good place to live in?'

'I'm not sure. It will be very hot by the middle of April. And you won't be able to stay with me, Ruskin—not at first, anyway, not until I can get married quarters and then, only if your mother returns... Meanwhile, you'll stay with your grandmother in Dehra.' He must have seen the disappointment in my face, because he quickly added, 'Of course, I'll come to see you often. Dehra isn't far from Delhi—only a night's train journey.'

But I was dismayed. It wasn't that I didn't want to stay with my grandmother, but I had grown so used to sharing my father's life and even watching him at work, that the thought of being separated from him was unbearable.

'Not as bad as going to boarding school,' he said. 'And that's the only alternative.'

'Not boarding school,' I said quickly, 'I'll run away from boarding school.'

'Well, you won't want to run away from your grandmother. She's very fond of you. And if you come with me to Delhi, you'll be alone all day in a stuffy little but while I'm away at work. Sometimes I may have to go on tour—then what happens?'

'I don't mind being on my own.' And this was true. I had already grown accustomed to having my own room and my own trunk and my own bookshelf and I felt as though I was about to lose these things.

'Will Ayah come too?' I asked.

My father looked thoughtful. 'Would you like that?'

'Ayah must come,' I said firmly. 'Otherwise I'll run away.'

'I'll have to ask her,' said my father.

Ayah, it turned out, was quite ready to come with us. In fact, she was indignant that Father should have considered leaving her behind. She had brought me up since my mother went away, and she wasn't going to hand over charge to any upstart aunt or governess. She was pleased and excited at the prospect of the move, and this helped to raise my spirits.

'What is Dehra like?' I asked my father.

'It's a green place,' he said. 'It lies in a valley in the foothills of the Himalayas, and it's surrounded by forests. There are lots of trees in Dehra.'

'Does grandmother's house have trees?'

'Yes. There's a big jackfruit tree in the garden. Your grandmother planted it when I was a boy. And there's an old banyan tree, which is good to climb. And there are fruit trees, litchis, mangoes, papayas.'

'Are there any books?'

'Grandmother's books won't interest you. But I'll be bringing you books from Delhi whenever I come to see you.'

I was beginning to look forward to the move. Changing houses had always been fun. Changing towns ought to be fun, too.

A few days before we left, I went to say goodbye to the Rani.

'I'm going away,' I said.

'How lovely!' said the Rani. 'I wish I could go away!'

'Why don't you?'

'They won't let me. They're afraid to let me out of the palace.'

'What are they afraid of, Your Highness?'

'That I might run away. Run away, far, far away, to the land where the leopards are learning to pray.'

Gosh, I thought, she's really quite crazy... But then she was silent, and started smoking a small hookah.

She drew on the hookah, looked at me, and asked, 'Where is your mother?'

'I haven't one.'

'Everyone has a mother. Did yours die?'

'No. She went away.'

She drew on her hookah again and then said, very sweetly, 'Don't go away...'

'I must,' I said. 'It's because of the war.'

'What war? Is there a war on? You see, no one tells me anything.'

'It's between us and Hitler,' I said.

'And who is Hitler?'

'He's a German.'

'I knew a German once, Dr Schreinherr, he had beautiful hands.'

'Was he an artist?'

'He was a dentist.'

The Rani got up from her couch and accompanied me out on to the balcony. When we looked down at the garden, we could see Dukhi weeding a flower bed. Both of us gazed down at him in silence, and I wondered what the Rani would say if I asked her if she had ever been in love with the palace gardener. Ayah had told me it would be an insulting question, so I held my peace. But as I walked slowly down the spiral staircase, the Rani's voice came after me.

'Thank him,' she said. 'Thank him for the beautiful rose.'

# WOULD ASTLEY RETURN?

The house was called 'Undercliff' because that's where it stood—under a cliff. The man who went away—the owner of the house—was Robert Astley. And the man who stayed behind—the old family retainer was Prem Bahadur.

Astley had been gone many years. He was still a bachelor in his late thirties when he'd suddenly decided that he wanted adventure, romance and faraway places. And he'd given the keys of the house to Prem Bahadur who'd served the family for thirty years—and had set off on his travels.

Someone saw him in Sri Lanka. He'd been heard of in Burma around the ruby mines at Mogok. Then he turned up in Java seeking a passage through the Sunda Straits. After that the trail petered out. Years passed. The house in the hill station remained empty.

But Prem Bahadur was still there, living in an outhouse.

Every day he opened up Undercliff, dusted the furniture in all the rooms, made sure that the bedsheets and pillowcases were clean and set out Astley's dressing gown and slippers.

In the old days, whenever Astley had come home after a journey or a long tramp in the hills, he had liked to bathe and change into his gown and slippers, no matter what the hour. Prem Bahadur still kept them ready. He was convinced that

Robert would return one day.

Astley himself had said so.

'Keep everything ready for me, Prem, old chap. I may be back after a year, or two years, or even longer, but I'll be back, I promise you. On the first of every month I want you to go to my lawyer, Mr Kapoor. He'll give you your salary and any money that's needed for the rates and repairs. I want you to keep the house tip-top!'

'Will you bring back a wife, sahib?'

'Lord, no! Whatever put that idea in your head?'

'I thought, perhaps—because you wanted the house kept ready...'

'Ready for me, Prem. I don't want to come home and find the old place falling down.'

And so Prem had taken care of the house—although there was no news from Astley. What had happened to him? The mystery provided a talking point whenever local people met on the Mall. And in the bazaar the shopkeepers missed Astley because he had been a man who spent freely.

His relatives still believed him to be alive. Only a few months back a brother had turned up—a brother who had a farm in Canada and could not stay in India for long. He had deposited a further sum with the lawyer and told Prem to carry on as before. The salary provided Prem with his few needs. Moreover, he was convinced that Robert would return.

Another man might have neglected the house and grounds, but not Prem Bahadur. He had a genuine regard for the absent owner. Prem was much older—now almost sixty and none too strong, suffering from pleurisy and other chest troubles—but he remembered Robert as both a boy and a young man. They had been together on numerous hunting and fishing trips in the mountains. They had slept out under the stars, bathed in icy mountain streams, and eaten from the same cooking pot. Once, when crossing a small river, they had been swept downstream by a flash flood, a wall of water that came thundering down the gorges without any warning during the rainy season. Together they had struggled back to safety. Back in the hill station, Astley told everyone that Prem had saved his life while Prem was equally insistent that he owed his life to Robert.

This year the monsoon had begun early and ended late. It dragged on through most of September and Prem Bahadur's cough grew worse and his breathing more difficult.

He lay on his charpoy on the veranda, staring out at the garden, which was beginning to get out of hand, a tangle of dahlias, snake lilies and convolvulus. The sun finally came out. The wind shifted from the southwest to the northwest and swept the clouds away. Prem Bahadur had shifted his charpoy into the garden and was lying in the sun, puffing at his small hookah, when he saw Robert Astley at the gate.

He tried to get up but his legs would not oblige him. The hookah slipped from his hand.

Astley came walking down the garden path and stopped in front of the old retainer, smiling down at him. He did not look a day older than when Prem Bahadur had last seen him.

'So you have come at last,' said Prem.

'I told you I'd return.'

'It has been many years. But you have not changed.'

'Nor have you, old chap.'

'I have grown old and sick and feeble.'

'You'll be fine now. That's why I've come.'

'I'll open the house,' said Prem and this time he found himself getting up quite easily.

'It isn't necessary,' said Astley.

'But all is ready for you!'

'I know. I have heard of how well you have looked after everything. Come then, let's take a last look around. We cannot stay, you know.'

Prem was a little mystified but he opened the front door and took Robert through the drawing room and up the stairs to the bedroom. Robert saw the dressing gown and the slippers and he placed his hand gently on the old man's shoulder.

When they returned downstairs and emerged into the sunlight Prem was surprised to see himself—or rather his skinny body—stretched out on the charpoy. The hookah was on the ground, where it had fallen.

Prem looked at Astley in bewilderment.

'But who is that—lying there?'

'It was you. Only the husk now, the empty shell. This is the real you, standing here beside me.'

'You came for me?'

'I couldn't come until you were ready. As for me, I left my shell a long time ago. But you were determined to hang on, keeping this house together. Are you ready now?'

'And the house?'

'Others will live in it. But come, it's time to go fishing.' Astley took Prem by the arm, and they walked through the dappled sunlight under the deodars and finally left that place forever.

# A LONG WALK FOR BINA

A leopard, lithe and sinewy, drank at the mountain stream, and then lay down on the grass to bask in the late February sunshine. Its tail twitched occasionally and the animal appeared to be sleeping. At the sound of distant voices it raised its head to listen, then stood up and leapt lightly over the boulders in the stream, disappearing among the trees on the opposite bank.

A minute or two later, three children came walking down the forest path. They were a girl and two boys, and they were singing in their local dialect an old song they had learnt from their grandparents.

> *Five more miles to go!*
> *We climb through rain and snow.*
> *A river to cross...*
> *A mountain to pass...*
> *Now we've four more miles to go!*

Their school satchels looked new, their clothes had been washed and pressed. Their loud and cheerful singing startled a spotted forktail. The bird left its favourite rock in the stream and flew down the dark ravine.

'Well, we have only three more miles to go,' said the bigger boy, Prakash, who had been this way hundreds of times. 'But first we have to cross the stream.'

He was a sturdy twelve-year-old with eyes like black currants and a mop of bushy hair that refused to settle down on his head. The girl and her small brother were taking this path for the first time.

'I'm feeling tired, Bina,' said the little boy.

Bina smiled at him, and Prakash said, 'Don't worry, Sonu, you'll get used to the walk. There's plenty of time.' He glanced at the old watch he'd been given by his grandfather. It needed constant winding. 'We can rest here for five or six minutes.'

They sat down on a smooth boulder and watched the clear water of the shallow stream tumbling downhill. Bina examined the old watch on Prakash's wrist. The glass was badly scratched and she could barely make out the figures on the dial. 'Are you sure it still gives the right time?' she asked.

'Well, it loses five minutes every day, so I put it ten minutes ahead at night. That means by morning it's quite accurate! Even our teacher, Mr Mani, asks me for the time. If he doesn't ask, I tell him! The clock in our classroom keeps stopping.'

They removed their shoes and let the cold mountain water run over their feet. Bina was the same age as Prakash. She had pink cheeks, soft brown eyes, and hair that was just beginning to lose its natural curls. Hers was a gentle face, but a determined little chin showed that she could be a strong person. Sonu, her younger brother, was ten. He was a thin boy who had been sickly as a child but was now beginning to fill out. Although he did not look very athletic, he could run like the wind.

◆

Bina had been going to school in her own village of Koli, on the other side of the mountain. But it had been a primary school, finishing at Class 5. Now, in order to study in Class 6, she would have to walk several miles every day to Nauti, where there was a high school going up to Class 8. It had been decided that Sonu would also shift to the new school, to give Bina company. Prakash, their neighbour in Koli, was already a pupil at the Nauti school. His mischievous nature, which sometimes got him into trouble, had resulted in his having to repeat a year.

But this didn't seem to bother him. 'What's the hurry?' he had told his indignant parents. 'You're not sending me to a foreign land when I finish school. And our cows aren't running away, are they?'

'You would prefer to look after the cows, wouldn't you?' asked Bina, as they got up to continue their walk.

'Oh, school's all right. Wait till you see old Mr Mani. He always gets our names mixed up, as well as the subjects he's supposed to be teaching. At our last lesson, instead of maths, he gave us a geography lesson!'

'More fun than maths,' said Bina.

'Yes, but there's a new teacher this year. She's very young they say, just out of college. I wonder what she'll be like.'

Bina walked faster and Sonu had some trouble keeping up with them. She was excited about the new school and the prospect of different surroundings. She had seldom been outside her own village, with its small school and single ration shop. The day's routine never varied—helping her mother in the fields or with household tasks like fetching water from the spring or cutting grass and fodder for the cattle. Her father, who was a soldier, was away for nine months in the year and Sonu was still too small for the heavier tasks.

As they neared Nauti Village, they were joined by other

children coming from different directions. Even where there were no major roads, the mountains were full of little lanes and shortcuts. Like a game of snakes and ladders, these narrow paths zigzagged around the hills and villages, cutting through fields and crossing narrow ravines until they came together to form a fairly busy road along which mules, cattle and goats joined the throng.

Nauti was a fairly large village, and from here a broader but dustier road started for Tehri. There was a small bus, several trucks and (for part of the way) a road roller. The road hadn't been completed because the heavy diesel roller couldn't take the steep climb to Nauti. It stood on the roadside halfway up the road from Tehri.

Prakash knew almost everyone in the area, and exchanged greetings and gossip with other children as well as with muleteers, bus drivers, milkmen and labourers working on the road. He loved telling everyone the time, even if they weren't interested.

'It's nine o'clock,' he would announce, glancing at his wrist. 'Isn't your bus leaving today?'

'Off with you!' the bus driver would respond, 'I'll leave when I'm ready.'

As the children approached Nauti, the small flat school buildings came into view on the outskirts of the village, fringed by a line of long-leaved pines. A small crowd had assembled on the one playing field. Something unusual seemed to have happened. Prakash ran forward to see what it was all about. Bina and Sonu stood aside, waiting in a patch of sunlight near the boundary wall.

Prakash soon came running back to them. He was bubbling over with excitement.

'It's Mr Mani!' he gasped. 'He's disappeared! People are

saying a leopard must have carried him off!'

II

Mr Mani wasn't really old. He was about fifty-five and was expected to retire soon. But for the children, most adults over forty seemed ancient! And Mr Mani had always been a bit absent-minded, even as a young man.

He had gone out for his early morning walk, saying he'd be back by eight o'clock, in time to have his breakfast and be ready for class. He wasn't married, but his sister and her husband stayed with him. When it was past nine o'clock his sister presumed he'd stopped at a neighbour's house for breakfast (he loved tucking into other people's breakfast) and that he had gone on to school from there. But when the school bell rang at ten o'clock, and everyone but Mr Mani was present, questions were asked and guesses were made.

No one had seen him return from his walk and enquiries made in the village showed that he had not stopped at anyone's house. For Mr Mani to disappear was puzzling; for him to disappear without his breakfast was extraordinary.

Then a milkman returning from the next village said he had seen a leopard sitting on a rock on the outskirts of the pine forest. There had been talk of a cattle-killer in the valley, of leopards and other animals being displaced by the construction of a dam. But as yet no one had heard of a leopard attacking a man. Could Mr Mani have been its first victim? Someone found a strip of red cloth entangled in a blackberry bush and went running through the village showing it to everyone. Mr Mani had been known to wear red pyjamas. Surely he had been seized and eaten! But where were his remains? And why had he been in his pyjamas?

Meanwhile Bina and Sonu and the rest of the children had

followed their teachers into the school playground. Feeling a little lost, Bina looked around for Prakash. She found herself facing a dark, slender young woman wearing spectacles, who must have been in her early twenties—just a little too old to be another student. She had a kind, expressive face and she seemed a little concerned by all that had been happening.

Bina noticed that she had lovely hands; it was obvious that the new teacher hadn't milked cows or worked in the fields!

'You must be new here,' said the teacher, smiling at Bina. 'And is this your little brother?'

'Yes, we've come from Koli Village. We were at school there.'

'It's a long walk from Koli. You didn't see any leopards, did you? Well, I'm new too. Are you in the sixth class?'

'Sonu is in the third. I'm in the sixth.'

'Then I'm your new teacher. My name is Tania Ramola. Come along, let's see if we can settle down in our classroom.'

◆

Mr Mani turned up at twelve o'clock, wondering what all the fuss was about. No, he snapped, he had not been attacked by a leopard; and yes, he had lost his pyjamas and would someone kindly return them to him?

'How did you lose your pyjamas, sir?' asked Prakash.

'They were blown off the washing line!' snapped Mr Mani.

After much questioning, Mr Mani admitted that he had gone further than he had intended, and that he had lost his way coming back. He had been a bit upset because the new teacher, a slip of a girl, had been given charge of the sixth, while he was still with the fifth, along with that troublesome boy Prakash, who kept on reminding him of the time! The Headmaster had explained that as Mr Mani was due to retire at the end of the year, the school did not wish to burden him with a senior class.

But Mr Mani looked upon the whole thing as a plot to get rid of him. He glowered at Miss Ramola whenever he passed her. And when she smiled back at him, he looked the other way!

Mr Mani had been getting even more absent-minded of late—putting on his shoes without his socks, wearing his homespun waistcoat inside out, mixing up people's names and, of course, eating other people's lunches and dinners. His sister had made a mutton broth for the postmaster, who was down with 'flu', and had asked Mr Mani to take it over in a thermos. When the postmaster opened the thermos, he found only a few drops of broth at the bottom—Mr Mani had drunk the rest somewhere along the way.

When sometimes Mr Mani spoke of his coming retirement, it was to describe his plans for the small field he owned just behind the house. Right now, it was full of potatoes, which did not require much looking after; but he had plans for growing dahlias, roses, French beans, and other fruits and flowers.

The next time he visited Tehri, he promised himself, he would buy some dahlia bulbs and rose cuttings. The monsoon season would be a good time to put them down. And meanwhile, his potatoes were still flourishing.

III

Bina enjoyed her first day at the new school. She felt at ease with Miss Ramola, as did most of the boys and girls in her class. Tania Ramola had been to distant towns such as Delhi and Lucknow—places they had only heard about—and it was said that she had a brother who was a pilot and flew planes all over the world. Perhaps he'd fly over Nauti some day!

Most of the children had of course seen planes flying overhead, but none of them had seen a ship, and only a few had been on a train. Tehri mountain was far from the railway and hundreds of miles from the sea. But they all knew about the big dam that was being built at Tehri, just forty miles away.

Bina, Sonu and Prakash had company for part of the way home, but gradually the other children went off in different directions. Once they had crossed the stream, they were on their own again.

It was a steep climb all the way back to their village. Prakash had a supply of peanuts which he shared with Bina and Sonu, and at a small spring they quenched their thirst.

When they were less than a mile from home, they met a postman who had finished his round of the villages in the area and was now returning to Nauti.

'Don't waste time along the way,' he told them. 'Try to get home before dark.'

'What's the hurry?' asked Prakash, glancing at his watch. 'It's only five o'clock.'

'There's a leopard around. I saw it this morning, not far from the stream. No one is sure how it got here. So don't take any chances. Get home early.'

'So, there really is a leopard,' said Sonu.

They took his advice and walked faster, and Sonu forgot to complain about his aching feet.

They were home well before sunset.

There was a smell of cooking in the air and they were hungry.

'Cabbage and roti,' said Prakash gloomily. 'But I could eat anything today.' He stopped outside his small slate-roofed house, and Bina and Sonu waved goodbye and carried on across a couple of ploughed fields until they reached their small stone house.

'Stuffed tomatoes,' said Sonu, sniffing just outside the front door.

'And lemon pickle,' said Bina, who had helped cut, sun and

salt the lemons a month previously.

Their mother was lighting the kitchen stove. They greeted her with great hugs and demands for an immediate dinner. She was a good cook who could make even the simplest of dishes taste delicious. Her favourite saying was, 'Home-made bread is better than roast meat abroad,' and Bina and Sonu had to agree.

Electricity had yet to reach their village, and they took their meal by the light of a kerosene lamp. After the meal, Sonu settled down to do a little homework, while Bina stepped outside to look at the stars.

Across the fields, someone was playing a flute. 'It must be Prakash,' thought Bina. 'He always breaks off on the high notes.' But the flute music was simple and appealing, and she began singing softly to herself in the dark.

## IV

Mr Mani was having trouble with the porcupines. They had been getting into his garden at night and digging up and eating his potatoes. From his bedroom window—left open now that the mild April weather had arrived—he could listen to them enjoying the vegetables he had worked hard to grow. Scrunch, scrunch! katar, katar, as their sharp teeth sliced through the largest and juiciest of potatoes. For Mr Mani it was as though they were biting through his own flesh. And the sound of them digging industriously as they rooted up those healthy, leafy plants made him tremble with rage and indignation. The unfairness of it all!

Yes, Mr Mani hated porcupines. He prayed for their destruction, their removal from the face of the earth. But, as his friends were quick to point out, 'The creator made porcupines too,' and in any case you could never see the creatures or catch them, they were completely nocturnal.

Mr Mani got out of bed every night, torch in one hand,

a stout stick in the other but, as soon as he stepped into the garden, the crunching and digging stopped and he was greeted by the most infuriating of silences. He would grope around in the dark, swinging wildly with the stick, but not a single porcupine was to be seen or heard. As soon as he was back in bed, the sounds would start all over again—scrunch, scrunch, katar, katar...

Mr Mani came to his class tired and dishevelled, with rings under his eyes and a permanent frown on his face. It took some time for his pupils to discover the reason for his misery, but when they did, they felt sorry for their teacher and took to discussing ways and means of saving his potatoes from the porcupines.

It was Prakash who came up with the idea of a moat or water ditch. 'Porcupines don't like water,' he said knowledgeably.

'How do you know?' asked one of his friends.

'Throw water on one and see how it runs! They don't like getting their quills wet.'

There was no one who could disprove Prakash's theory, and the class fell in with the idea of building a moat, especially as it meant getting most of the day off.

'Anything to make Mr Mani happy,' said the Headmaster, and the rest of the school watched with envy as the pupils of Class 5, armed with spades and shovels collected from all parts of the village, took up their positions around Mr Mani's potato field and began digging a ditch.

By evening the moat was ready, but it was still dry and the porcupines got in again that night and had a great feast.

'At this rate,' said Mr Mani gloomily, 'there won't be any potatoes left to save.'

But the next day, Prakash and the other boys and girls managed to divert the water from a stream that flowed past the village. They had the satisfaction of watching it flow gently into the ditch. Everyone went home in a good mood. By nightfall, the ditch had overflowed, the potato field was flooded, and Mr Mani found himself trapped inside his house. But Prakash and his friends had won the day. The porcupines stayed away that night!

◆

A month had passed, and wild violets, daisies and buttercups now sprinkled the hill slopes and, on her way to school, Bina gathered enough to make a little posy. The bunch of flowers fitted easily into an old ink well. Miss Ramola was delighted to find this little display in the middle of her desk.

'Who put these here?' she asked in surprise.

Bina kept quiet, and the rest of the class smiled secretively. After that, they took turns bringing flowers for the classroom.

On her long walks to school and home again, Bina became aware that April was the month of new leaves. The oak leaves were bright green above and silver beneath, and when they rippled in the breeze they were clouds of silvery green. The path was strewn with old leaves, dry and crackly. Sonu loved kicking them around.

Clouds of white butterflies floated across the stream. Sonu was chasing a butterfly when he stumbled over something dark and repulsive. He went sprawling on the grass. When he got to his feet, he looked down at the remains of a small animal.

'Bina! Prakash! Come quickly!' he shouted.

It was part of a sheep, killed some days earlier by a much larger animal.

'Only a leopard could have done this,' said Prakash.

'Let's get away, then,' said Sonu. 'It might still be around!'

'No, there's nothing left to eat. The leopard will be hunting elsewhere by now. Perhaps it's moved on to the next valley.'

'Still, I'm frightened,' said Sonu. 'There may be more leopards!'

Bina took him by the hand. 'Leopards don't attack humans!' she said.

'They will, if they get a taste for people!' insisted Prakash.

'Well, this one hasn't attacked any people as yet,' said Bina, although she couldn't be sure. Hadn't there been rumours of a leopard attacking some workers near the dam? But she did not want Sonu to feel afraid, so she did not mention the story. All she said was, 'It has probably come here because of all the activity near the dam.'

All the same, they hurried home. And for a few days, whenever they reached the stream, they crossed over very quickly, unwilling to linger too long at that lovely spot.

V

A few days later, a school party was on its way to Tehri to see the new dam that was being built.

Miss Ramola had arranged to take her class, and Mr Mani, not wishing to be left out, insisted on taking his class as well. That meant there were about fifty boys and girls taking part in the outing. The little bus could only take thirty. A friendly truck driver agreed to take some children if they were prepared to sit on sacks of potatoes. And Prakash persuaded the owner of the diesel roller to turn it around and head it back to Tehri—with him and a couple of friends up on the driving seat.

Prakash's small group set off at sunrise, as they had to walk some distance in order to reach the stranded road roller. The bus left at 9 a.m. with Miss Ramola and her class, and Mr Mani and some of his pupils. The truck was to follow later.

It was Bina's first visit to a large town, and her first bus ride. The sharp curves along the winding, downhill road made several children feel sick. The bus driver seemed to be in a tearing hurry. He took them along at a rolling, rollicking speed, which made Bina feel quite giddy. She rested her head on her arms and refused to look out of the window. Hairpin bends and cliff edges, pine forests and snow-capped peaks, all swept past her, but she felt too ill to want to look at anything. It was just as well—those sudden drops, hundreds of feet to the valley below, were quite frightening. Bina began to wish that she hadn't come—or that she had joined Prakash on the road roller instead!

Miss Ramola and Mr Mani didn't seem to notice the lurching and groaning of the old bus. They had made this journey many times. They were busy arguing about the advantages and disadvantages of large dams—an argument that was to continue on and off for much of the day.

Meanwhile, Prakash and his friends had reached the roller. The driver hadn't turned up, but they managed to reverse it and get it going in the direction of Tehri. They were soon overtaken by both bus and truck but kept moving along at a steady chug. Prakash spotted Bina at the window of the bus and waved cheerfully. She responded feebly.

Bina felt better when the road levelled out near Tehri. As they crossed an old bridge over the wide river, they were startled by a loud bang which made the bus shudder. A cloud of dust rose above the town.

'They're blasting the mountain,' said Miss Ramola.

'End of a mountain,' said Mr Mani, mournfully.

While they were drinking cups of tea at the bus stop, waiting for the potato truck and the road roller, Miss Ramola and Mr Mani continued their argument about the dam. Miss Ramola maintained that it would bring electric power and water for irrigation to large areas of the country, including the surrounding area. Mr Mani declared that it was a menace, as it was situated in an earthquake zone. There would be a terrible disaster if the dam burst! Bina found it all very confusing. And what about the animals in the area, she wondered, what would happen to them?

The argument was becoming quite heated when the potato truck arrived. There was no sign of the road roller, so it was decided that Mr Mani should wait for Prakash and his friends while Miss Ramola's group went ahead.

◆

Some eight or nine miles before Tehri, the road roller had broken down, and Prakash and his friends were forced to walk. They had not gone far, however, when a mule train came along—five or six mules that had been delivering sacks of grain in Nauti. A boy rode on the first mule, but the others had no loads.

'Can you give us a ride to Tehri?' called Prakash.

'Make yourselves comfortable,' said the boy.

There were no saddles, only gunny sacks strapped on to the mules with rope. They had a rough but jolly ride down to the Tehri bus stop. None of them had ever ridden mules; but they had saved at least an hour on the road.

Looking around the bus stop for the rest of the party, they could find no one from their school. And Mr Mani, who should have been waiting for them, had vanished.

VI

Tania Ramola and her group had taken the steep road to the hill above Tehri. Half an hour's climbing brought them to a little plateau which overlooked the town, the river and the dam site.

The earthworks for the dam were only just coming up, but a wide tunnel had been bored through the mountain to divert the river into another channel. Down below, the old town was still spread out across the valley and from a distance it looked quite charming and picturesque.

'Will the whole town be swallowed up by the waters of the dam?' asked Bina.

'Yes, all of it,' said Miss Ramola. 'The clock tower and the old palace. The long bazaar, and the temples, the schools and the jail, and hundreds of houses, for many miles up the valley. All those people will have to go—thousands of them! Of course they'll be resettled elsewhere.'

'But the town's been here for hundreds of years,' said Bina. 'They were quite happy without the dam, weren't they?'

'I suppose they were. But the dam isn't just for them—it's for the millions who live further downstream, across the plains.'

'And it doesn't matter what happens to this place?'

'The local people will be given new homes somewhere else.' Miss Ramola found herself on the defensive and decided to change the subject. 'Everyone must be hungry. It's time we had our lunch.'

Bina kept quiet. She didn't think the local people would want to go away. And it was a good thing, she mused, that there was only a small stream and not a big river running past her village. To be uprooted like this—a town and hundreds of villages—and put down somewhere on the hot, dusty plains—seemed to her unbearable.

'Well, I'm glad I don't live in Tehri,' she said.

She did not know it, but all the animals and most of the birds had already left the area. The leopard had been among them.

◆

They walked through the colourful, crowded bazaar, where fruit sellers did business beside silversmiths, and pavement vendors sold everything from umbrellas to glass bangles. Sparrows attacked sacks of grain, monkeys made off with bananas, and stray cows and dogs rummaged in refuse bins, but nobody took any notice. Music blared from radios. Buses blew their horns. Sonu bought a whistle to add to the general din, but Miss Ramola told him to put it away. Bina had kept five rupees aside, and now she used it to buy a cotton headscarf for her mother.

As they were about to enter a small restaurant for a meal, they were joined by Prakash and his companions; but of Mr Mani there was still no sign.

'He must have met one of his relatives,' said Prakash. 'He has relatives everywhere.'

After a simple meal of rice and lentils, they walked the length of the bazaar without finding Mr Mani. At last, when they were about to give up the search, they saw him emerge from a by-lane, a large sack slung over his shoulder.

'Sir, where have you been?' asked Prakash. 'We have been looking for you everywhere.'

On Mr Mani's face was a look of triumph.

'Help me with this bag,' he said breathlessly.

'You've bought more potatoes, sir,' said Prakash.

'Not potatoes, boy. Dahlia bulbs!'

## VII

It was dark by the time they were all back in Nauti. Mr Mani had refused to be separated from his sack of dahlia bulbs, and had been forced to sit in the back of the truck with Prakash and most of the boys.

Bina did not feel so ill on the return journey. Going uphill was definitely better than going downhill! But by the time the bus reached Nauti it was too late for most of the children to walk back to the more distant villages. The boys were put up in different homes, while the girls were given beds in the school veranda.

The night was warm and still. Large moths fluttered around the single bulb that lit the veranda. Counting moths, Sonu soon fell asleep. But Bina stayed awake for some time, listening to the sounds of the night. A nightjar went tonk-tonk in the bushes, and somewhere in the forest an owl hooted softly. The sharp call of a barking deer travelled up the valley from the direction of the stream. Jackals kept howling. It seemed that there were more of them than ever before.

Bina was not the only one to hear the barking deer. The leopard, stretched full length on a rocky ledge, heard it too. The leopard raised its head and then got up slowly. The deer was its natural prey. But there weren't many left, and that was why the leopard, robbed of its forest by the dam, had taken to attacking dogs and cattle near the villages.

As the cry of the barking deer sounded nearer, the leopard left its lookout point and moved swiftly through the shadows towards the stream.

VIII

In early June the hills were dry and dusty, and forest fires broke out, destroying shrubs and trees, killing birds and small animals. The resin in the pines made these trees burn more fiercely, and the wind would take sparks from the trees and carry them into the dry grass and leaves, so that new fires would spring up before the old ones had died out. Fortunately, Bina's village was not in the pine belt; the fires did not reach it. But Nauti was surrounded by a fire that raged for three days, and the children had to stay away from school.

And then, towards the end of June, the monsoon rains arrived and there was an end to forest fires. The monsoon lasts three months and the lower Himalayas would be drenched in rain, mist and cloud for the next three months.

The first rain arrived while Bina, Prakash and Sonu were returning home from school. Those first few drops on the dusty path made them cry out with excitement. Then the rain grew heavier and a wonderful aroma rose from the earth.

'The best smell in the world!' exclaimed Bina.

Everything suddenly came to life. The grass, the crops, the trees, the birds. Even the leaves of the trees glistened and looked new.

That first wet weekend, Bina and Sonu helped their mother plant beans, maize and cucumbers. Sometimes, when the rain was very heavy, they had to run indoors. Otherwise they worked in the rain, the soft mud clinging to their bare legs.

Prakash now owned a dog, a black dog with one ear up and one ear down. The dog ran around getting in everyone's way, barking at cows, goats, hens and humans, without frightening any of them. Prakash said it was a very clever dog, but no one else seemed to think so. Prakash also said it would protect the village from the leopard, but others said the dog would be the first to be taken—he'd run straight into the jaws of Mr Spots!

In Nauti, Tania Ramola was trying to find a dry spot in the quarters she'd been given. It was an old building and the roof was leaking in several places. Mugs and buckets were scattered about the floor in order to catch the drips.

Mr Mani had dug up all his potatoes and presented them to the friends and neighbours who had given him lunches and dinners. He was having the time of his life, planting dahlia bulbs all over his garden.

'I'll have a field of many-coloured dahlias!' he announced. 'Just wait till the end of August!'

'Watch out for those porcupines,' warned his sister. 'They

eat dahlia bulbs too!'

Mr Mani made an inspection tour of his moat, no longer in flood, and found everything in good order. Prakash had done his job well.

◆

Now, when the children crossed the stream, they found that the water level had risen by about a foot. Small cascades had turned into waterfalls. Ferns had sprung up on the banks. Frogs chanted.

Prakash and his dog dashed across the stream. Bina and Sonu followed more cautiously. The current was much stronger now and the water was almost up to their knees. Once they had crossed the stream, they hurried along the path, anxious not to be caught in a sudden downpour.

By the time they reached school, each of them had two or three leeches clinging to their legs. They had to use salt to remove them. The leeches were the most troublesome part of the rainy season. Even the leopard did not like them. It could not lie in the long grass without getting leeches on its paws and face.

One day, when Bina, Prakash and Sonu were about to cross the stream they heard a low rumble, which grew louder every second. Looking up at the opposite hill, they saw several trees shudder, tilt outwards and begin to fall. Earth and rocks bulged out from the mountain, then came crashing down into the ravine.

'Landslide!' shouted Sonu.

'It's carried away the path,' said Bina. 'Don't go any further.'

There was a tremendous roar as more rocks, trees and bushes fell away and crashed down the hillside.

Prakash's dog, who had gone ahead, came running back, tail between his legs.

They remained rooted to the spot until the rocks had stopped falling and the dust had settled. Birds circled the area, calling wildly. A frightened barking deer ran past them.

'We can't go to school now,' said Prakash. 'There's no way around.'

They turned and trudged home through the gathering mist.

In Koli, Prakash's parents had heard the roar of the landslide. They were setting out in search of the children when they saw them emerge from the mist, waving cheerfully.

IX

They had to miss school for another three days, and Bina was afraid they might not be able to take their final exams. Although Prakash was not really troubled at the thought of missing exams, he did not like feeling helpless just because their path had been swept away. So he explored the hillside until he found a goat-track going around the mountain. It joined up with another path near Nauti. This made their walk longer by a mile, but Bina did not mind. It was much cooler now that the rains were in full swing.

The only trouble with the new route was that it passed close to the leopard's lair. The animal had made this area its own since being forced to leave the dam area.

One day Prakash's dog ran ahead of them barking furiously. Then he ran back whimpering.

'He's always running away from something,' observed Sonu. But a minute later he understood the reason for the dog's fear.

They rounded a bend and Sonu saw the leopard standing in their way. They were struck dumb—too terrified to run. It was a strong, sinewy creature. A low growl rose from its throat. It seemed ready to spring.

They stood perfectly still, afraid to move or say a word.

And the leopard must have been equally surprised. It stared at them for a few seconds, then bounded across the path and into the oak forest.

Sonu was shaking. Bina could hear her heart hammering. Prakash could only stammer: 'Did you see the way he sprang? Wasn't he beautiful?'

He forgot to look at his watch for the rest of the day.

A few days later, Sonu stopped and pointed to a large outcrop of rock on the next hill.

The leopard stood far above them, outlined against the sky. It looked strong, majestic. Standing beside it were two young cubs.

'Look at those little ones!' exclaimed Sonu.

'So it's a female, not a male,' said Prakash.

'That's why she was killing so often,' said Bina. 'She had to feed her cubs too.'

They remained still for several minutes, gazing up at the leopard and her cubs. The leopard family took no notice of them.

'She knows we are here,' said Prakash, 'but she doesn't care. She knows we won't harm them.'

'We are cubs too!' said Sonu.

'Yes,' said Bina. 'And there's still plenty of space for all of us. Even when the dam is ready there will still be room for leopards and humans.'

X

The school exams were over. The rains were nearly over too. The landslide had been cleared, and Bina, Prakash and Sonu were once again crossing the stream.

There was a chill in the air, for it was the end of September.

Prakash had learnt to play the flute quite well, and he played on the way to school and then again on the way home. As a result he did not look at his watch so often. One morning they found a small crowd in front of Mr Mani's house.

'What could have happened?' wondered Bina. 'I hope he hasn't got lost again.'

'Maybe he's sick,' said Sonu.

'Maybe it's the porcupines,' said Prakash.

But it was none of these things.

Mr Mani's first dahlia was in bloom, and half the village had turned up to look at it! It was a huge red double dahlia, so heavy that it had to be supported with sticks. No one had ever seen such a magnificent flower!

Mr Mani was a happy man. And his mood only improved over the coming week, as more and more dahlias flowered— crimson, yellow, purple, mauve, white—button dahlias, pom-pom dahlias, spotted dahlias, striped dahlias... Mr Mani had them all! A dahlia even turned up on Tania Ramola's desk—he got along quite well with her now—and another brightened up the Headmaster's study.

A week later, on their way home—it was almost the last day of the school term—Bina, Prakash and Sonu talked about what they might do when they grew up.

'I think I'll become a teacher,' said Bina. 'I'll teach children about animals and birds, and trees and flowers.'

'Better than maths!' said Prakash.

'I'll be a pilot,' said Sonu. 'I want to fly a plane like Miss Ramola's brother.'

'And what about you, Prakash?' asked Bina.

Prakash just smiled and said, 'Maybe I'll be a flute player,' and he put the flute to his lips and played a sweet melody.

'Well, the world needs flute players too,' said Bina, as they fell into step beside him.

The leopard had been stalking a barking deer. She paused when she heard the flute and the voices of the children. Her own young ones were growing quickly, but the girl and the two boys did not look much older.

They had started singing their favourite song again.

*Five more miles to go!*
*We climb through rain and snow,*
*A river to cross...*
*A mountain to pass...*
*Now we've four more miles to go!*

The leopard waited until they had passed, before returning to the trail of the barking deer.

# GRANDFATHER'S EARTHQUAKE

'If ever there's a calamity,' Grandmother used to say, 'it will find Grandfather in his bath.' Grandfather loved his bath—which he took in a large, round aluminium tub. He sometimes spent as long as an hour in the tub, 'wallowing' as he called it, and splashing around like a boy.

He was in his bath during the earthquake that convulsed Bengal and Assam on 12 June 1897—an earthquake so severe that even today the region of the great Brahmaputra River basin hasn't settled down. Not long ago it was reported that the entire Shillong Plateau had moved an appreciable distance away from the Brahmaputra towards the Bay of Bengal. According to the Geological Survey of India, this shift has been taking place gradually over almost a hundred years.

Had Grandfather been alive, he would have added one more clipping to his scrapbook on the earthquake. The clipping goes in anyway, because the scrapbook is now with his children. More than newspaper accounts of the disaster, it was Grandfather's own letters and memoirs that made the earthquake seem recent and vivid; for he, along with Grandmother and two of their children (one of them my father), was living in Shillong, then a picturesque little hill station in Assam, when the earth shook and the mountains heaved.

As I have mentioned, Grandfather was in his bath, splashing about, and did not hear the first rumbling. But Grandmother was in the garden, hanging out or taking in the washing (she could never remember which) when, suddenly, the animals began making a hideous noise—a sure intimation of a natural disaster, for animals sense the approach of an earthquake much more quickly than humans.

The crows all took wing, wheeling wildly overhead and cawing loudly. The chickens flapped in circles, as if they were being chased. Two dogs sitting on the veranda suddenly jumped up and ran out with their tails between their legs. Within half a minute of her noticing the noise made by the animals, Grandmother heard a rattling, rumbling noise, like the approach of a train.

The noise increased for about a minute, and then there was the first trembling of the ground. The animals by this time all seemed to have gone mad. Treetops lashed backwards and forwards, doors banged and windows shook, and Grandmother swore later that the house actually swayed in front of her. She had difficulty standing straight, though this could have been due more to the trembling of her knees than to the trembling of the ground.

The first shock lasted for about a minute and a half. 'I was in my tub having a bath,' Grandfather wrote for posterity, 'which for the first time in the last two months I had taken in the afternoon instead of in the morning. My wife and children and the ayah were downstairs. Then the shock came, accompanied by a loud rumbling sound under the earth and a quaking which increased in intensity every second. It was like putting so many shells in a basket, and shaking them up with a rapid sifting motion from side to side.

'At first I did not realize what it was that caused my tub

to sway about and the water to splash. I rose up, and found the earth heaving, while the washstand, basin, ewer, cups and glasses danced and rocked about in the most hideous fashion. I rushed to the inner door to open it and search for my wife and children, but could not move the dratted door as boxes, furniture and plaster had come up against it. The back door was the only way of escape. I managed to burst it open, and, thank God, was able to get out. Sections of the thatched roof had slithered down on the four sides like a pack of cards and blocked all the exits and entrances.

'With only a towel wrapped around my waist, I ran out into the open to the front of the house, but found only my wife there. The whole front of the house was blocked by the fallen section of thatch from the roof. Through this I broke my way under the iron railings and extricated the others. The bearer had pluckily borne the weight of the whole thatched roof section on his back as it had slithered down, and in this way saved the ayah and children from being crushed beneath it.'

After the main shock of the earthquake had passed, minor shocks took place at regular intervals of five minutes or so, all through the night. But during that first shake-up the town of Shillong was reduced to ruin and rubble. Everything made of masonry was brought to the ground. Government House, the post office, the jail, all tumbled down. When the jail fell, the prisoners, instead of making their escape, sat huddled on the road waiting for the superintendent to come to their aid.

Wrote a young girl in a newspaper called *The Englishman*, 'The ground began to heave and shake. I stayed on my bicycle for a second, and then fell off and got up and tried to run, staggering about from side to side of the road. To my left I saw great clouds of dust, which I afterwards discovered to be houses falling and the earth slipping from the sides of the hills.

To my right I saw the small dam at the end of the lake torn asunder and the water rushing out, the wooden bridge across the lake break in two and the sides of the lake falling in; and at my feet the ground cracking and opening. I was wild with fear and didn't know which way to turn.'

The lake rose up like a mountain, and then totally disappeared, leaving only a swamp of red mud. Not a house was left standing. People were rushing about, wives looking for husbands, parents looking for children, not knowing whether their loved ones were alive or dead. A crowd of people had collected on the cricket ground, which was considered the safest place; but Grandfather and the family took shelter in a small shop on the road outside his house. The shop was a rickety wooden structure, which had always looked as though it would fall down in a strong wind. But it withstood the earthquake.

And then the rain came, and it poured. This was extraordinary, because before the earthquake there wasn't a cloud to be seen; but, five minutes after the shock, Shillong was enveloped in cloud and mist. The shock was felt for more than a hundred miles on the Assam–Bengal Railway. A train was overturned at Shamshernagar; another was derailed at Mantolla. Over a thousand people lost their lives in the Cherrapunji Hills, and in other areas, too, the death toll was heavy.

The Brahmaputra burst its banks and many cultivators were drowned in the flood. A tiger was found drowned. And in North Bhagalpur, where the earthquake started, two elephants sat down in the bazaar and refused to get up until the following morning.

Over a hundred men who were at work in Shillong's government printing press were caught in the building when it collapsed, and, though the men of a Gurkha regiment did splendid rescue work, only a few were brought out alive. One of those killed in Shillong was Mr McCabe, a British official. Grandfather described the ruins of Mr McCabe's house: 'Here a bedpost, there a sword, a broken desk or chair, a bit of torn carpet, a well-known hat with its Indian Civil Service colours, battered books, all speaking reminiscences of the man we mourn.'

While most houses collapsed where they stood, Government House, it seems, 'fell backwards'. The church was a mass of red stones in ugly disorder. The organ was a tortured wreck.

A few days later, the family and other refugees were making their way to Calcutta to stay with friends or relatives. It was a slow, tedious journey, with many interruptions, for the roads and railway lines had been badly damaged and passengers had often to be transported in trolleys. Grandfather was rather struck by the stoicism displayed by an assistant engineer. At one station a telegram was handed to the engineer informing him that his bungalow had been destroyed. 'Beastly nuisance,' he observed with an aggrieved air. 'I've seen it cave in during a storm, but this is the first time it has played me such a trick on account of an earthquake.'

The family got to Calcutta to find the inhabitants of the capital in a panic; for they too had felt the quake and were expecting it to recur. The damage in Calcutta was slight compared to the devastation elsewhere, but nerves were on edge, and people slept in the open or in carriages. Cracks and fissures had appeared in a number of old buildings, and Grandfather was among the many who were worried at the proposal to fire a salute of sixty guns on Jubilee Day (the Diamond Jubilee of Queen Victoria); they felt the gunfire would bring down a number of shaky buildings. Obviously, Grandfather did not wish to be caught in his bath a second time. However, Queen Victoria was not to be deprived of her salute. The guns were duly fired, and Calcutta remained standing.

# A MAGIC OIL

One cosy summer morning in Fosterganj, when not much was happening, but life was going on just the same, I was in the bank, run by Vishaal (manager), Negi (cashier), and Suresh (peon). I was sitting opposite Vishaal, who was at his desk, on which there were two handsome paperweights but no papers. Suresh had brought me a cup of tea from the tea shop across the road. There was just one customer in the bank, Hassan, who was making a deposit.

In walked Foster. He'd made an attempt at shaving, but appeared to have given up at a crucial stage, because now he looked like a wasted cricketer finally on his way out. The effect was enhanced by the fact that he was wearing flannel trousers that had once been white but were now greenish yellow; the previous monsoon was to blame. He had found an old tie, and this was strung around his neck or rather his unbuttoned shirt collar. The said shirt had seen many summers and winters in Fosterganj, and was frayed at the cuffs. Even so, Foster looked quite spry, as compared to when I had last seen him.

'Come in, come in!' said Vishaal, always polite to his customers, even those who had no savings. 'How is your gladioli farm?'

'Coming up nicely,' said Foster. 'I'm growing potatoes too.'

'Very nice. But watch out for the porcupines, they love potatoes.'

'Shot one last night. Cut my hands getting the quills out. But porcupine meat is great. I'll send you some the next time I shoot one.'

'Well, keep some ammunition for the leopard. We've got to get it before it kills someone else.'

'It won't be around for two or three weeks. They keep moving, do leopards. He'll circle the mountain, then be back in these parts. But that's not what I came to see you about, Mr Vishaal. I was hoping for a small loan.'

'Small loan, big loan, that's what we are here for. In what way can we help you, sir?'

'I want to start a chicken farm.'

'Most original.'

'There's a great shortage of eggs in Mussoorie. The hotels want eggs, the schools want eggs, the restaurants want eggs. And they have to get them from Rajpur or Dehradun.'

'Hassan has a few hens,' I put in.

'Only enough for home consumption. I'm thinking in terms of hundreds of eggs—and broiler chickens for the table. I want to make Fosterganj the chicken capital of India. It will be like old times, when my ancestor planted the first potatoes here, brought all the way from Scotland!'

'I thought they came from Ireland,' I said. 'Captain Young, up at Landour.'

'Oh well, we brought other things. Like Scotch whisky.'

'Actually, Irish whisky got here first. Captain Kennedy, up in Simla.' I wasn't Irish, but I was in a combative frame of mind, which is the same as being Irish.

To mollify Foster, I said, 'You did bring the bagpipe.' And when he perked up, I added, 'But the Gurkha is better at playing it.'

This contretemps over, Vishaal got Foster to sign a couple of forms and told him that the loan would be processed in due course and that we'd all celebrate over a bottle of Scotch whisky. Foster left the room with something of a swagger. The prospect of some money coming in—even if it is someone else's—will put any man in an optimistic frame of mind. And for Foster the prospect of losing it was as yet far distant.

I wanted to make a phone call to my bank in Delhi, so that I could have some of my savings sent to me, and Vishaal kindly allowed me to use his phone.

There were only four phones in all of Fosterganj, and there didn't seem to be any necessity for more. The bank had one. So did Dr Bisht. So did Brigadier Bakshi, retired. And there was one in the police station, but it was usually out of order.

The police station, a one room affair, was manned by a daroga and a constable. If the daroga felt like a nap, the constable took charge. And if the constable took the afternoon off, the daroga would run the place. This worked quite well, as there wasn't much crime in Fosterganj—if you didn't count Foster's illicit still at the bottom of the hill (Scottish hooch, he called the stuff he distilled); or a charming young delinquent called Sunil, who picked pockets for a living (though not in Fosterganj); or the barber who supplemented his income by supplying charas to his agents at some of the boarding schools; or the man who sold the secretions of certain lizards, said to increase sexual potency— except that it was only linseed oil, used for oiling cricket bats.

I found the last mentioned, a man called Rattan Lal, sitting on a stool outside my door when I returned from the bank.

'Saande-ka-tel,' he declared abruptly, holding up a small bottle containing a vitreous yellow fluid. 'Just one application, sahib, and the size and strength of your valuable member will increase dramatically. It will break down doors, should doors be shut on you. No chains will hold it down. You will be as a stallion, rampant in a field full of fillies. Sahib, you will rule the roost! Memsahibs and beautiful women will fall at your feet.'

'It will get me into trouble, for certain,' I demurred. 'It's great stuff, I'm sure. But wasted here in Fosterganj.'

Rattan Lal would not be deterred. 'Sahib, every time you try it, you will notice an increase in dimensions, guaranteed!'

'Like Pinocchio's nose,' I said in English. He looked puzzled. He understood the word 'nose', but had no idea what I meant.

'Naak?' he said. 'No, sahib, you don't rub it on your nose. Here, down between the legs,' and he made as if to give a demonstration. I held a hand up to restrain him.

'There was a boy named Pinocchio in a far-off country,' I explained, switching back to Hindi. 'His nose grew longer every time he told a lie.'

'I tell no lies, sahib. Look, my nose is normal. Rest is very big. You want to see?'

'Another day,' I said.

'Only ten rupees.'

'The bottle or the rest of you?'

'You joke, sahib,' he said, and thrust a bottle into my unwilling hands and removed a ten-rupee note from my shirt pocket; all done very simply.

'I will come after a month and check-up,' he said. 'Next time I will bring the saanda itself! You are in the prime of your life, it will make you a bull among men.' And away he went.

◆

The little bottle of oil stood unopened on the bathroom shelf for weeks. I was too scared to use it. It was like the bottle in *Alice's Adventures in Wonderland* with the label DRINK ME.

Alice drank it, and shot up to the ceiling. I wasn't sure I

wanted to grow that high.

I did wonder what would happen if I applied some of it to my scalp. Would it stimulate hair growth? Would it stimulate my thought processes? Put an end to writer's block?

Well, I never did find out. One afternoon I heard a clatter in the bathroom and looked in to see a large and sheepish-looking monkey jump out of the window with the bottle.

But to return to Rattan Lal—some hours after I had been sold the aphrodisiac, I was walking up to town to get a newspaper when I met him on his way down.

'Any luck with the magic oil?' I asked.

'All sold out!' he said, beaming with pleasure. 'Ten bottles sold at the Savoy, and six at Hakman's. What a night it's going to be for them.' And he rubbed his hands at the prospect.

'A very busy night,' I said. 'Either that, or they'll be looking for you to get their money back.'

'I'll be back next month. If you are still here, I'll keep another bottle for you. Look there!' He took me by the arm and pointed to a large rock lizard that was sunning itself on the parapet. 'You catch me some of those, and I'll pay you for them. Be my partner. Bring me lizards—not small ones, only big fellows—and I will buy!'

'How do you extract the tel?' I asked.

'Ah, that's a trade secret. But I will show you when you bring me some saandas. Now I must go. My good wife waits for me with impatience.'

And off he went, down the bridle path to Rajpur.

The rock lizard was still on the wall, enjoying its afternoon siesta.

As I wasn't making much as a writer, it did occur to me that I might make a living from breeding rock lizards. Perhaps Vishaal would give me a loan.

# THE TAIL OF THE LIZARD

There was a break in the rains, the clouds parted, and the moon appeared—a full moon, bathing the mountains in a pollen-yellow light. Little Fosterganj, straddling the slopes of the Ganga-Yamuna watershed, basked in the moonlight, each lighted dwelling a firefly in the night.

Only Fairy Glen Palace was unlit, brooding in the darkness. I was returning from an evening show at the Rialto in Mussoorie. It had been a long walk, but a lovely one. I stopped outside the palace gate, wondering about its lonely inhabitants and all that might have happened within its walls...

I reached Hassan's bakery around midnight, and mounted the steps to my room. My door was open. It was never locked, as I had absolutely nothing that anyone would want to take away. The typewriter, which I had hired from a shop in Dehradun, was a heavy machine, designed for office use; no one was going to carry it off.

But someone was in my bed.

Fast asleep. Snoring peacefully. Not Goldilocks. Nor a bear. I switched on the light, shook the recumbent figure. He started up. It was Sunil. After giving him a beating, the police had let him go.

'Uncle, you frightened me!' he exclaimed.

He called me 'Uncle', although I was only some fifteen or sixteen years older than him. Call a tiger 'Uncle' and he won't harm you; or so the forest dwellers say. Not quite sure how it works out with people approaching middle age. Being addressed as 'Uncle' didn't make me very fond of Sunil.

'I'm the one who should be frightened,' I said. 'A pickpocket in my bed!'

'I don't pick pockets any more, Uncle. I've turned over a new leaf. Don't you know that expression?'

Sunil had studied up to Class 8 in a 'convent school'.

'Well, you can turn out of my bed,' I said. 'And return that watch you took off me before you got into trouble.'

'You lent me the watch, Uncle. Don't you remember? Here!' He held out his arm. 'Take it back.' There were two watches on his wrist; my modest HMT and something far more expensive.

I removed the HMT and returned it to my own wrist.

'Now, can I have my bed back?' I asked.

'There's room for both of us.'

'No, there isn't, it's only a khatiya. It will collapse under our combined weight. But there's this nice easy chair here, and in the morning, when I get up, you can have the bed.'

Reluctantly, Sunil got off the bed and moved over to the cane chair. Perhaps I'd made a mistake. It meant that Sunil would be awake all night, and that he'd want to talk. Nothing can be more irritating than a room companion who talks all night.

I switched off the light and stretched out on the cot. It was a bit wobbly. Perhaps the floor would have been better. Sunil sat in the chair, whistling and singing film songs—something about a red dupatta blowing in the wind, and telephone calls from Rangoon to Dehradun. A romantic soul, Sunil, when he wasn't picking pockets. Did I say there's nothing worse than a companion who talks all night? I was wrong. Even worse is a companion who sings all night.

'You can sing in the morning,' I said. 'When the sun comes out. Now go to sleep.'

There was silence for about two minutes. Then: 'Uncle?'

'What is it?'

'I have to turn over a new leaf.'

'In the morning, Sunil,' I turned over and tried to sleep.

'Uncle, I have a *project*.'

'Well, don't involve me in it.'

'It's all seedha-saadha, and very interesting. You know that old man who sells saande-ka-tel—the oil that doubles your manhood?'

'I haven't tried it. It's an oil taken from a lizard, isn't it?'

'A big lizard.'

'So?'

'Well, he's old now and can't go hunting for these lizards. You can only find them in certain places.'

'Maybe he should retire and do something else, then. Grow marigolds. Their oil is also said to be good for lovers.'

'Not as good as lizard oil.'

'So what's your project?' He was succeeding in keeping me awake. 'Are you going to gather lizards for him?'

'Exactly, Uncle. Why don't you join me?'

◆

Next morning Sunil elaborated on his scheme. I was to finance the tour. We would trek, or use a bus where there were roads, and visit the wooded heights and rocky slopes above the Bhagirathi River, on its descent from the Gangotri Glacier. We would stay in rest houses, dharamsalas, or small hotels. We would locate those areas where the monitors, or large rock lizards were plentiful, catch as many as possible and bring them back alive to Fosterganj, where our gracious mentor would reward us to the tune of two hundred rupees per reptile. Sunil and I would share this bonanza.

Although I had idly considered doing something similar, now that I thought about it it didn't seem like it stood any chance of succeeding. But I was bored, and it sounded like it could be fun, even an adventure of sorts, and I would have Sunil as guide, philosopher and friend.

He could be a lovely and happy-go-lucky companion— provided he kept his hands out of other people's pockets and did not sing at night.

Hassan was equally sceptical about the success of the project. For one thing, he did not believe in the magical properties of saande-ka-tel (never having felt the need for it); and, for another, he did not think those lizards would be caught so easily. But he thought it would be a good thing for Sunil, something different from what he was used to doing. The young man might benefit from my 'intellectual' company. And, in the hills, not many folks had money in their pockets.

And so, with the blessings of Hassan, and a modest overdraft from Vishaal, our friendly bank manager, I packed a haversack with essentials (including my favourite ginger biscuits as prepared by Hassan) and set out with Sunil on the old pilgrim road to Tehri and beyond.

Sunil had brought along two large baskets, as receptacles for the lizards when captured. But as he had no intention of carrying them himself—and wisely refrained from asking me to do so—he had brought along a twelve-year-old youth from the bazaar—a squint-eyed, hare-lipped, one-eared character called Buddhoo, whose intelligence and confidence made up for his looks. Buddhoo was to act as our porter and general factotum. On our outward journey he had only to carry the two empty baskets; Sunil hadn't told him what their eventual contents might be.

It was late July, still monsoon time, when we set out on the Tehri road.

In those days it was still a mule-track, meandering over several spurs and ridges, before descending to the big river. It was about forty miles to Tehri. From there we could get a bus, at least up to Pratap Nagar, the old summer capital of the hill state.

◆

That first day on the road was rather trying. I had done a certain amount of walking in the hills, and I was reasonably fit. Sunil, for all his youth, had never walked further than Mussoorie's cinemas or Dehra's railway station, where the pickings for his agile fingers had always been good. Buddhoo, on the other hand, belied his short stature by being so swift of foot that he was constantly leaving us far behind. Every time we rounded a corner, expecting to find him waiting for us, he would be about a hundred yards ahead, never tiring, never resting.

To keep myself going I would sing either Harry Lauder's 'Keep right on to the end of the road,' or Nelson Eddy's 'Tramp, tramp, tramp'.

> *Tramp, tramp, tramp, along the highway,*
> *Tramp, tramp, tramp, the road is free!*
> *Blazing trails along the byways...*

Sunil did not appreciate my singing.

'You don't sing well,' he said. 'Even those mules are getting nervous.' He gestured at a mule-train that was passing us on the narrow path. A couple of mules were trying to break away from the formation.

'Nothing to do with my singing,' I said. 'All they want are those young bamboo shoots coming up on the hillside.'

Sunil asked one of the mule-drivers if he could take a ride on a mule; anything to avoid trudging along the stony path. The mule-driver agreeing, Sunil managed to mount one of the beasts and went cantering down the road, leaving us far behind.

Buddhoo waited for me to catch up. He pointed at a large rock to the side of road, and there, sure enough, resting at ease, basking in the morning sunshine, was an ungainly monitor lizard about the length of my forearm.

'Too small,' said Buddhoo, who seemed to know something about lizards. 'Bigger ones higher up.'

The lizard did not move. It stared at us with a beady eye; a contemptuous sort of stare, almost as if it did not think very highly of humans. I wasn't going to touch it. Its leathery skin looked uninviting; its feet and tail reminded me of a dinosaur; its head was almost serpent like. Who would want to use its body secretions, I wondered. Certainly not if they had seen the creature. But human beings, men especially, will do almost anything to appease their vanity. Tiger's whiskers or saande-ka-tel—anything to improve their sagging manhood.

We did not attempt to catch the lizard. Sunil was supposed to be the expert. And he was already a mile away, enjoying his mule-ride.

An hour later he was sitting on the grassy verge, nursing a sore backside. Riding a mule can take the skin off the backside of an inexperienced rider.

'I'm in pain,' he complained. 'I can't get up.'

'Use saande-ka-tel,' I suggested.

Buddhoo went sauntering up the road, laughing to himself.

'He's mad,' said Sunil.

'That makes three of us, then.'

♦

By noon we were hungry. Hassan had provided us with buns and biscuits, but these were soon finished, and we were longing for a real meal. Late afternoon we trudged into Dhanolti, a scenic spot with great views of the snow peaks; but we were in no mood for scenery. Who can eat sunsets? A forest rest house was the only habitation, and had food been available we could have spent the night there. But the caretaker was missing. A large black dog frightened us off.

So on we tramped, three small dots on a big mountain, mere specks, beings of no importance. In creating this world, God showed that he was a great mathematician; but in creating man, he got his algebra wrong. Puffed up with self-importance, we are in fact the most dispensable of all his creatures.

On a long journey, the best companion is usually the one who talks the least, and in that way Buddhoo was a comforting presence. But I wanted to know him better.

'How did you lose your ear?' I asked.

'Bear tore it off,' he said, without elaborating.

Brevity is the soul of wit, or so they say.

'Must have been painful,' I ventured.

'Bled a lot.'

'I wouldn't care to meet a bear.'

'Lots of them out here. If you meet one, run downhill. They don't like running downhill.'

'I'll try to remember that,' I said, grateful for his shared wisdom. We trudged on in silence. To the south, the hills were bleak and windswept; to the north, moist and well-forested.

The road ran along the crest of the ridge, and the panorama it afforded, with the mountains striding away in one direction and the valleys with their gleaming rivers snaking their way towards the plains, gave me an immense feeling of freedom. I doubt if Sunil felt the same way. He was preoccupied with tired legs and a sore backside. And for Buddhoo it was a familiar scene.

A brief twilight, and then, suddenly, it grew very dark. No moon; the stars just beginning to appear. We rounded a bend, and a light shone from a kerosene lamp swinging outside a small roadside hut.

It was not the pilgrim season, but the owner of the hut was ready to take in the odd traveller. He was a grizzled old man. Over the years the wind had dug trenches in his cheeks and forehead. A pair of spectacles, full of scratches, almost opaque, balanced on a nose long since broken. He'd lived a hard life. A survivor.

'Have you anything to eat?' demanded Sunil.

'I can make you dal-bhaat,' said the shopkeeper. Dal and rice was the staple diet of the hills; it seldom varied.

'Fine,' I said. 'But first some tea.'

The tea was soon ready, hot and strong, the way I liked it. The meal took some time to prepare, but in the meantime we made ourselves comfortable in a corner of the shop, the owner having said we could spend the night there. It would take us two hours to reach the township of Chamba, he said. Buddhoo concurred. He knew the road.

We had no bedding, but the sleeping area was covered with old sheepskins stitched together, and they looked comfortable enough. Sunil produced a small bottle of rum from his shoulder bag, unscrewed the cap, took a swig, and passed it around. The old man declined. Buddhoo drank a little; so did I. Sunil polished off the rest. His eyes became glassy and unfocused.

'Where did you get it?' I asked.

'Hassan Uncle gave it to me.'

'Hassan doesn't drink—he doesn't keep it, either.'

'Actually, I picked it up in the police station, just before they let me go. Found it in the havildar's coat pocket.'

'Congratulations,' I said. 'He'll be looking forward to seeing you again.'

The dal-bhaat was simple but substantial.

'Could do with some pickle,' grumbled Sunil, and then fell asleep before he could complain any further.

◆

We were all asleep before long. The sheepskin rug was reasonably comfortable. But we were unaware that it harboured a life of its own—a miniscule but active population of fleas and bugs—dormant when undisturbed, but springing into activity at the proximity of human flesh and blood.

Within an hour of lying down we were wide awake.

When God, the Great Mathematician, discovered that in making man he had overdone things a bit, he created the bedbug to even things out.

Soon I was scratching. Buddhoo was up and scratching. Sunil came out of his stupor and was soon cursing and scratching. The fleas had got into our clothes, the bugs were feasting on our blood. When the world as we know it comes to an end, these will be the ultimate survivors.

Within a short time we were stomping around like Kathakali dancers. There was no relief from the exquisite torture of being seized upon by hundreds of tiny insects thirsting for blood or body fluids.

The tea shop owner was highly amused. He had never seen such a performance—three men cavorting around the room, scratching, yelling, hopping around.

And then it began to rain. We heard the first heavy raindrops pattering a rhythm on the tin roof. They increased in volume, beating against the only window and bouncing off the banana fronds in the little courtyard. We needed no urging. Stripping off our clothes, we dashed outside, naked in the wind and rain, embracing the elements. What relief! We danced in the rain until it stopped, and then, getting back into our clothes with some reluctance, we decided to be on our way, no matter how dark or forbidding the night.

We paid for our meal—or rather, I paid for it, being the only one in funds—and bid goodnight and goodbye to our host. Actually, it was morning, about 2 a.m., but we had no intention of bedding down again; not on those sheepskin rugs.

A half-moon was now riding the sky. The rain had refreshed us. We were no longer hungry. We set out with renewed vigour.

Great lizards, beware!

◆

At daybreak we tramped into the little township of Chamba, where Buddhoo proudly pointed out a memorial to soldiers from the area who had fallen fighting in the trenches in France during World War I. His grandfather had been one of them. Young men from the hills had traditionally gone into the army; it was the only way they could support their families; but times were changing, albeit slowly. The towns now had several hopeful college students. If they did not find jobs they could go into politics.

The motor road from Rishikesh passed through Chamba, and we were able to catch a country bus which deposited us at Pratap Nagar later that day.

Pratap Nagar is not on the map, but it used to be a place of some consequence once upon a time. Back in the days of the old Tehri Raj it had been the raja's summer capital. There had even been a British resident and a tiny European population—

just a handful of British officials and their families. But after Independence, the raja no longer had any use for the place. The state had been poor and backward, and over the years he had spent more time in Dehradun and Mussoorie.

We were there purely by accident, having got into the wrong bus at Chamba.

The wrong bus or the wrong train can often result in interesting consequences. It's called the charm of the unexpected.

Not that Pratap Nagar was oozing with charm. A dilapidated palace, an abandoned courthouse, a dispensary without a doctor, a school with a scatter of students and no teachers, and a marketplace selling sad-looking cabbages and cucumbers—these were the sights and chief attractions of the town. But I have always been drawn to decadent, decaying, forgotten places— Fosterganj being one of them—and while Sunil and Buddhoo passed the time chatting to some of the locals at the bus stand— which appeared to be the centre of all activity—I wandered off along the narrow, cobbled lanes until I came to a broken wall.

Passing through a break in the wall I found myself in a small cemetery. It contained a few old graves. The inscriptions had worn away from most of the tombstones, and on others the statuary had been damaged. Obviously no one had been buried there for many years.

In one corner I found a grave that was better preserved than the others, by virtue of the fact that the lettering had been cut into an upright stone rather than a flat slab. It read:

> *Dr Robert Hutchinson*
> *Physician to His Highness*
> *Died July 13, 1933*
> *of Typhus Fever*
> *May his soul rest in peace.*

Typhus fever! I had read all about it in an old medical dictionary published half a century ago by *The Statesman* of Calcutta and passed on to me by a fond aunt. Not to be confused with typhoid, typhus fever is rare today but sometimes occurs in overcrowded, unsanitary conditions and is definitely spread by lice, ticks, fleas, mites and other microorganisms thriving in filthy conditions—such as old sheepskin rugs which have remained unwashed for years.

I began to scratch at the very thought of it.

I remembered more: 'Attacks of melancholia and mania sometimes complicate the condition, which is often fatal.'

Needless to say, I now found myself overcome by a profound feeling of melancholy. No doubt the mania would follow.

I examined the other graves, and found one more victim of typhus fever. There must have been an epidemic. Fortunately for my peace of mind, the only other decipherable epitaph told of a missionary lady who had fallen victim to an earthquake in 1905. Somehow, an earthquake seemed less sinister than a disease brought on by bloodthirsty bugs.

While I was standing there, ruminating on matters of life and death, my companions turned up, and Sunil exclaimed, 'Well done, Uncle, you've already found one!'

I hadn't found anything, being somewhat shortsighted, but Sunil was pointing across to the far wall where a great fat lizard sat basking in the sun.

Its tail was as long as my arm. Its legs were spread sideways, like a goalkeeper's. Its head moved from side to side, and suddenly its tongue shot out and seized a passing dragonfly.

In seconds the beautiful insect was imprisoned in a pair of strong jaws.

The giant lizard consumed his lunch, then glanced at us standing a few feet away.

'Plenty of fat around that fellow,' observed Sunil. 'Full of that precious oil!'

The lizard let out a croak, as though it had something to say on the matter. But Sunil wasn't listening. He lunged forward and grabbed the lizard by its tail. Miraculously, the tail came away in his hands.

Away went the lizard, minus its tail.

Buddhoo was doubled up with laughter. 'The tail's no use,' he said. 'Nothing in the tail!'

Sunil flung the tail away in disgust.

'Never mind,' I said. 'Catch a lizard by its tail—make a wish, it cannot fail!'

'Is that true?' asked Sunil, who had a superstitious streak.

'Nursery rhyme from Brazil,' I said.

The lizard had disappeared, but a white-bearded patriarch was looking at us from over the wall.

'You need a net,' he said. 'Catching them by hand isn't easy. Too slippery.'

We thanked him for his advice; said we'd go looking for a net.

'Maybe a bedsheet will do,' Sunil said.

The patriarch smiled, stroked his flowing white beard, and asked, 'But what will you do with these lizards? Put them in a zoo?'

'It's their oil we want,' said Sunil, and made a sales pitch for the miraculous properties of saande-ka-tel.

'Oh, that,' said the patriarch, looking amused. 'It will irritate the membranes and cause some inflammation. I know—I'm a nature therapist. All superstition, my friends. You'll get the same effect, even better, with machine oil. Try sewing machine oil. At least it's harmless. Leave the poor lizards alone.'

And the barefoot mendicant hitched up his dhoti, gave us a friendly wave, and disappeared in the monsoon mist.

# STRYCHNINE IN THE COGNAC

*Sick was she on Thursday,*
*Dead was she on Friday,*
*Glad was Tom on Saturday night*
*To bury his wife on Sunday.*

Miss Bean was reclining in a cane chair in a corner of the hotel's Beer Garden, reciting old nursery rhymes to herself, when Mr Lobo, the resident pianist, walked over and placed a glass of lemon juice beside her.

'Oranges and lemons,' he said, sitting down beside her. 'Which do you prefer?'

'Both,' she said. 'Oranges for the complexion, lemons for the digestion.'

'Words of wisdom. But that nursery rhyme sounded a bit wicked. I can only remember the innocent ones like Jack and Jill.'

'Not so innocent. "Jack fell down and broke his crown"—he wouldn't have survived a broken head. Maybe Jill pushed him over a cliff—and went tumbling after!'

'Like the judge who fell into the Kempty Waterfall. Was he pushed, or did he fall?'

'We shall never know. No witnesses. But here comes the Roys—what a handsome couple!'

The Roys were, indeed, a handsome couple, as you would expect them to be. Dilip Roy was in his mid-forties, but still a name to be reckoned with in Bollywood. He was greying a little at the temples, just below the edges of his wig; but he remained lean and athletic looking, and the meaty, romantic roles still came his way. His wife, Rosie Roy, was two or three years younger than him, but inclined to plumpness. When she was in her later twenties and early thirties she had starred in several very popular films—two of them opposite Dilip Roy, whom she had married while on location with him in Kashmir—but of late she had been having some difficulty in getting parts to her liking. She hadn't been feeling very well and had taken to sleeping late in the mornings. Her doctor had suspected diabetes and had advised a complete check-up, but she kept putting off the necessary tests.

'You need change,' said Dilip, always concerned about her health. 'A change from Bombay. A fortnight in the hills will do wonders for you. I'll spend a few days with you too, before I start shooting in Switzerland. Where would you like to go— Simla, Mussoorie, Darjeeling, Ooty?'

'Why not Switzerland?'

Dilip laughed uneasily. 'It wouldn't be much of a holiday. I'd be shooting all the time and you'd be pestered by hangers-on and loads of admirers.'

'Former admirers.'

'Well, better an old admirer than none at all. And I'm still jealous.'

They settled on Mussoorie—partly because Dilip Roy's father was an old friend of Nandu, the owner of the hotel, and partly because Rosie had spent an idyllic summer there as a girl, staying with an aunt in Barlowganj. When the couple arrived at the hotel, the first person they encountered was Miss

Bean, watering the potted aspidistras in the porch of the hotel.

'Hello,' said Rosie, smiling curiously at Miss Bean. 'Are you the new gardener?'

'I'm the old gardener,' said Miss Bean. 'A long-time resident, actually. But the gardener never waters these aspidistras—he thinks they are hardy enough to go without. But plants are like humans—they need a little attention from time to time, otherwise they die of neglect. I've seen you somewhere, haven't I?'

'Only if you go to the movies,' said Rosie. And added, 'Old movies.'

'You're Rosie Roy,' said Miss Bean. 'I saw you in *Cobra Lady*.'

'Wasn't it terrible?'

'It was so bad that I enjoyed every moment of it. And this must be the great Dilip Roy,' observed Miss Bean, as the well-known actor joined them, followed by room boys loaded with luggage. 'The hero of *Love in Kathmandu*,' said Miss Bean, but the hero ignored her.

Dilip Roy did not stop to gossip, but continued up the steps to the lobby, followed by his wife and the room boys. Miss Bean gave her attention to the aspidistras.

'Friendly heroine but not so friendly hero,' she said to the nearest potted plant. The aspidistra appeared to agree.

◆

The couple settled in, and over the next few days Miss Bean saw quite a lot of them although she took care not to intrude in any way, for it was obvious that the Roys were not looking for company.

In the evenings Dilip Roy would plant himself on a bar stool, and work his way through several whiskies, occasionally answering polite questions from the bartender or a casual customer, but always rather morosely, his mind obviously elsewhere. In the background, Mr Lobo, the hotel pianist, would play popular numbers but without receiving any encouragement or applause.

Rosie did not join her husband in the bar. But occasionally a Martini was served to her in her room—sometimes two Martinis—it was obvious that she liked a gin and vermouth cocktail now and then. Nandu presented her with a bottle of cognac, and she kept it on her dresser, intending to open it only when her husband was in the mood to drink with her.

They went out for quiet walks together, avoiding the Mall where they would quickly be recognized by both locals and visitors. Sometimes they passed Miss Bean, who was herself a great walker. As they were fellow residents of the hotel they would stop to exchange comments on the weather, the view, the hotel, the town, sometimes even the country and the rest of the world. But from the quiet of the mountains the rest of the world can seem very far away.

Rosie Roy liked the look of Miss Bean and was always ready to stop and talk. Dilip Roy was polite but brusque. The local gossip did not interest him, and he thought Miss Bean a rather quaint and rather foolish bit of flotsam surviving from the days of the British Raj. But then (as Rosie argued) the hotel, the cottages, the winding footpaths, the hill station itself, were all survivors of the Raj, and if their old-world atmosphere did not please you, it might have been better to holiday in Goa—and soak up the Portuguese atmosphere!

India would always be haunted by its history...

◆

One day the Roys had a violent quarrel. Miss Bean was no eavesdropper but she couldn't help overhearing every word that was spoken. Her favourite place was a bench situated behind a tall hibiscus hedge. It looked out upon the snows, and Miss Bean liked to spend a half hour there with a book while Fluff, her little terrier, investigated the hillside, looking for rats' holes. You couldn't see the bench from the Beer Garden, and it was in the Beer Garden that Rosie and Dilip Roy were confronting each other.

'You're off, because of that woman in Bandra.' Rosie's voice was quite shrill. 'A week away from her and you're beginning to look like a real Majnu—all pale and melancholy.'

'Don't make up things.' Dilip Roy sounded impatient rather than melancholy. 'You know they start shooting on the new film next week. And it's in Switzerland, not Bandra.'

'You're not the star. They can do without you. You've been getting too fat for leading roles. And you're drinking too much.'

'I'll end up an alcoholic if I stay here much longer. The doctors advised rest for you, not for me. You've given yourself ulcers and you won't get any better if you worry over trifles.'

Here the couple were interrupted by a group of youngsters seeking autographs, and Miss Bean took advantage of the diversion to slip away, taking a roundabout path to her room. Fluff enjoyed the extended walk.

That evening Dilip Roy opened the bottle of cognac. He was leaving the next morning, and he was in a mood to celebrate. But he was not particularly fond of cognac, and did most of his celebrating with his favourite Scotch. Rosie poured herself a glass of cognac, then put the bottle away on the dresser in their room. There it remained all night.

Dilip Roy breakfasted alone in the dining room, then sent for a taxi to take him down to Dehradun. Rosie did not see him off.

'She's sleeping late,' explained Dilip. 'She has a headache.

Don't disturb her.'

'Enjoy yourself in Switzerland,' said Nandu, the affable proprietor.

'Look after Rosie,' said Dilip Roy. 'Let her get plenty of rest.'

And everyone did their best to make Rosie comfortable and welcome, because she was much the more gracious of the two. The manager and staff fussed over her, and Mr Lobo played her favourite tunes, especially the one she always requested:

> *The future is hard to see,*
> *Whatever will be will be...*

Even Miss Bean was drawn towards Rosie and joined her on an inspection of the garden, for they were both fond of flowers, and in late summer the grounds were awash with bright yellow marigolds, petunias, larkspur and climbing roses. They had coffee together and Rosie recalled her parents and happy childhood days spent in Mussoorie; she did not talk about her marriage.

As evening came on, Rosie would retire to her room and send for a Martini; it would be followed by a second. She would have a light supper in her room—usually a chicken or mushroom soup with toast—followed by a few sips of cognac as a nightcap... and then to bed.

This routine continued for three or four days, and the cognac bottle was still half full because Rosie preferred Martinis. Dilip Roy made a couple of calls from Bombay—the crew would be off to Switzerland any day, and meanwhile they were shooting some scenes in Lonavala.

He had been away for almost a week when Rosie suddenly fell ill. At about ten o'clock after her dinner she rang her bell. A room boy answered her summons, found her on her bed, still dressed, and having a fit of sorts. He ran for the manager.

The manager hurried to the room, followed by a concerned Mr Lobo. They found her still having convulsions.

'I'll go get Dr Bisht,' said Lobo, and hurried from the room. Minutes later they heard the splutter of his scooter as he took the winding driveway down to the Mall. Dr Bisht had a scooter too—it was the Age of the Scooter—and he arrived in time to give Rosie some basic first aid and arrange for her to be taken to the local hospital. He was cautious in his diagnosis. 'Looks like food poisoning,' he said, and then his eye fell on the open bottle of cognac, of which about half remained. There was still some liquor in a glass, and he sniffed at it and made a face. 'Or something else... We'd better have this bottle examined.' But that would take time.

A call was put through to Dilip Roy's studio in Bombay; but the actor was in Switzerland, and air flights were not very frequent those days. It would be two or three days before he could return.

Miss Bean visited Rosie Roy every day, and so, occasionally, did Nandu and Mr Lobo. To everyone's relief and amazement, Rosie made a good recovery. There were crystals of strychnine at the bottom of that bottle, but they had only just begun to dissolve. Another evening's drinking and Rosie would have reached the fatal dose lying in wait for her. For it was obvious that someone had placed the poison in the bottle, and that someone could only have been Dilip Roy, before he had left Mussoorie. Far away at the time of his wife's expiry, he would have the perfect alibi.

Of course, nothing could be proven—all was surmise and conjecture—but Rosie was certain in her own mind that her husband had intended to do away with her in absentia, so to speak—and had very nearly succeeded.

She and Miss Bean had become fast friends, and Rosie found

herself confiding all her fears and suspicions to the older person, and turning to her for advice and guidance.

◆

They sat together on the lawns of the Savoy, Rosie reclining in an easy chair, Miss Bean quite at ease on a wooden bench. From indoors came the tinkle of a piano as Mr Lobo played 'September Song'. Miss Bean sang the words softly, almost to herself:

*But it's a long time from May to December,*
*And the days grown short when we reach September.*

'That's a pretty song,' said Rosie. 'A little sad, though.'

'September is a sad month,' said Miss Bean musingly. 'The end of summer, the end of all those lovely picnics. Holding hands and paddling in mountain streams. Hot sunny days. And then all that rain—weeks of endless rain and mist. September brings back the sunshine if only for a short time, and then those icy winds will start coming down from the snows.'

'How romantic!' exclaimed Rosie. 'You are lucky to have lived here most of your life. Well, perhaps I'll come and join you when I've finished with that wretched husband of mine in Bombay.'

'What do you intend to do, my dear? Put arsenic in his vodka?'

'Arsenic is too slow. But if he eats enough of those chocolate-coated hazelnuts of which he is so fond, he could well come to a sticky end.'

'What do you mean, dear?'

'This is only for your ears, Auntie May.'

She addressed Miss Bean by her first name whenever she became trustful and confiding. 'I know you won't give me away—just in case something happens.'

'What could happen now?'

'Well, during the last two years I've been so miserable that I've always kept a little cyanide pill with me, just so that I can put an end to my life if it becomes too unbearable.'

'Oh, dear. Do throw it away. Don't even think of doing away with yourself.'

'Well, actually I did throw it away—got rid of it. I took the pill and gave it a nice coating of chocolate and then mixed it up with all the little hazelnut chocolates in the tin that Dilip always carries around.'

'Oh, but that was wicked of you. Quite diabolical! Understandable though, when you think of what he tried to do to you. But he could get to that chocolate pill any day. Pop it into his mouth, and then—'

'Pop off?' added Rosie, a glint in her hazel eyes.

'But it's been some time, hasn't it? Almost three weeks since he left. Someone else might have helped himself or herself to a chocolate—'

Just then they saw Nandu advancing across the lawn. It wasn't his usual amble, he looked very purposeful.

'Bad news,' he said, when he reached their sunny corner. 'I've just had a call from Dilip's manager. Your husband died last night. Suicide, it appears. Cyanide. He must have been feeling very guilty about what happened to you. I'm sorry for your loss, Rosie...'

◆

That evening Miss Bean dined with Rosie in the old ballroom. It was the end of the season, and only a few tables were occupied. Mr Lobo was at the piano, playing nostalgic numbers.

'What will you have, Auntie May? You're my special guest

today. It's not that I want to celebrate or anything like that—'

'I quite understand, my dear.'

'So you must have a decent wine, instead of that dreadful crème-de-menthe you make in your room. Here's the wine list.'

Miss Bean ran her eye down the wine list. She was no blackmailer, but she couldn't help feeling a little surge of power as she made her choice. And it was such a long time since she'd enjoyed a really good wine. So she plumped for the most expensive wine on the list, and sat back in anticipation.

# WHEN THE CLOCK STRIKES THIRTEEN

Tick-tock,
Tick-tock.

One day that clock will strike thirteen and I'll be liberated forever, thought Rani Ma as the clock struck twelve and she poured herself another generous peg from the vodka bottle. Recently she had moved from gin to vodka, the latter seemed a little more suited to her mid-morning depression. The bottle was half empty but it would take her through to late afternoon when her ancient manservant, Bahadur, would arrive with another bottle and some vegetables for the evening meal. She did not bother with breakfast or lunch, and yet she was fat, fifty, and oh so forlorn.

Living alone on the seventh floor of a new apartment building—Ranipur's only skyscraper—had only emphasized Rani Ma's loneliness and isolation. Friends had drifted away over the years. Her selfish nature and acerbic tongue had destroyed many relationships. There were no children, for marriage had passed her by. Occasionally a nephew or cousin would turn up, hoping for a loan, but would go away disappointed.

Rani Ma had nothing to live for, and almost every day,

after the third vodka, she contemplated suicide. If only that clock would strike thirteen, Time for her would stop, and she would take that fatal leap into oblivion. Because it had to be a leap—something dramatic, something final. No sleeping tablets for her, no overdose of Alprax, no Hyoscine in her vodka. And she was far too clumsy to try slitting her own wrists, she'd only make a mess of it, and Bahadur would find her bleeding on the carpet and run for a doctor. There was an old shotgun in the bottom drawer of a cupboard but the box of cartridges that went with it looked damp and mouldy; of no use, except perhaps to frighten off an intruder. No, there was only one thing to do—leap off her seventh floor balcony, stay airborne for a few seconds, and then—oblivion!

Why wait for that clock to strike thirteen? Time would never stop—not for her, not for all those thousands below, hurrying about in a heat of hope, striving to find some meaning in their lives, some sustenance for their hordes of children; some happy, some miserable but alive...

She opened the door to her balcony and stood there, unsteady, supporting herself against the low railing. Down below on the busy street, cars, scooters, cyclists, pedestrians, went about their business unaware of the woman looking down upon them from her balcony. Once the queen of Ranipur, she had always looked down upon them. Now her rule extended no further than her apartment, and the world went by unheeding.

Tick-tock, tick-tock, why keep listening to that wretched clock? Time must have a stop.

◆

Walking along the pavement with a jaunty air, hat at an angle, humming an old tune, was Colonel Jolly, recently retired. He was on his way to the bank to collect his pension, and he enjoyed walking into town, nodding or waving to acquaintances, stopping occasionally to buy a paper or an ice cream, for he was still a boy as far as ice creams went. He was enjoying his retirement; his sons were settled abroad, his wife was at home baking a cake for his evening tea. He was in love with life and he hadn't a care in the world.

As he passed below the tall apartment building, something came between him and the sun, blocking out his vision. He had no idea what it was that struck him, bringing about a total eclipse. One moment he was striding along, at peace with the world; the next, he was flat on the pavement, buried beneath a mountain of flesh that had struck him like a comet.

Both the Colonel and Rani Ma were rushed to the nearest hospital. The Colonel's neck and spine had been shattered and he died without recovering consciousness. Rani Ma took some time to recover; but, thanks to her fall, having been cushioned by the poor Colonel, recover she did, retiring to a farmhouse on the outskirts of town.

Colonel Jolly, lover of life, had lost his to a cruel blow of fate. Rani Ma, who hated living, survived into a grumpy old age.

She is still waiting for the clock to strike thirteen.